BROKEN

POWERTOOLS: THE SHIELDS, BOOK 4

JAYNE RYLON

HAPPY ENDINGS PUBLISHING

V3

eBook ISBN: 978-1-947093-30-0

Print ISBN: 978-1-947093-31-7

Cover Design by Jayne Rylon

Editing by Mackenzie Walton

Proofreading by Fedora Chen

Formatting by Jayne Rylon

ABOUT THE BOOK

Geeky tech girls aren't supposed to have this much fun with their super spy co-workers.

Ruby typically supports a team of do-gooder assassins from the safety of her supercomputer in their command center. She's dragged into danger when hackers attack her, empty millions from her crypto wallet, and threaten the global economy by tampering with blockchain technology.

Worse, her attraction to two of the agents she works with —Ace and Liam—is a distraction none of them can afford, especially when she winds up sharing a bed with them for her own safety.

They've got issues of their own. Ace barely returned to active duty after a grievous injury that wrecked his arm and nearly ended his career. His wounds fractured more than bones, shaking Liam's confidence and willingness to deepen their partnership both on and off duty because they risk their lives daily to protect others. And that's before they admit that they're falling for the same nerdy-yet-adorable woman, who should also be strictly off-limits.

Can Ruby fix what's broken between the three of them before the hackers end her career and her life?

From New York Times and USA Today bestselling author Jayne Rylon comes a steamy new multi-partner standalone series set in the Powertools universe.

The Shields security team accepts missions in the grey area of both law and morality that no one else wants or can handle. They're a ragtag bunch of special ops soldiers, ex-government agents, and hackers wrangled by a former construction worker who aspired to be a superhero's sidekick when he grew up. What could go wrong?

ADDITIONAL INFORMATION

Sign up for the Naughty News for contests, release updates, news, appearance information, sneak peek excerpts, reading-themed apparel deals, and more. www.jaynerylon.com/newsletter

Shop for autographed books, reading-themed apparel, goodies, and more www.jaynerylon.com/shop

A complete list of Jayne's books can be found at www.jaynerylon.com/books

1

———

Ruby tapped her toe in time with the theme music of her favorite anime as it pumped through her bulky headphones. No silly earbuds for her, nope. When it came to tech she always craved the most powerful, top-of-the-line shit. Her fingers flew over her keyboard and her eyes darted from line to line of code flying past on the bank of a dozen monitors arranged around her in three layer semi-circle. There in the Shields command center—manning the supercomputer brains of their operation—she was in her happy place, surrounded by zeros and ones that painted a whole new reality away from the physical world.

She probably should have taken her friends up on a night out, but she knew Kennedy, Sola, and Laurel were looking forward to hanging out with their guys in the downtime between missions. And by hanging out she meant they were being spoiled to death in bed considering the three women had six boyfriends between them. And Ruby couldn't even find one!

Okay, so she'd have to leave her beloved megacomputer to land a guy. That felt like a lot of effort and she preferred her fuzzy Kurama character slippers to heels.

That didn't mean she didn't get lonely at times like this, when the rest of her team, who'd also become a cross between friends and family, had retreated to their own quarters upstairs for the night. Soon she'd switch to her personal workstation but her apartment seemed awfully isolated lately. Especially when her two smoking hot neighbors decided to get it on. Her fancy headphones muffled their moans, but it couldn't stop the wall between their apartments from quaking as they fucked against it.

Ruby swiped between applications, her palms growing a bit sweaty as she recalled the thuds, groans, and other noises penetrating the divider between their living spaces. She was certain Ace and Liam didn't realize she was aware they went at it most times they were alone together for more than five minutes. Nor did they have a clue about how many nights she'd pleasured herself while eavesdropping on them like a creeper or after waking from one of the wicked dreams they'd inspired her to have more and more often lately.

She fanned her face, then attempted to distract herself by checking out the upcoming House of Goblins NFT launch. Of course, she wasn't satisfied with public information. If Ruby dug a little deeper into the identities behind the online profiles posting the digital artwork for sale and their other holdings, she figured she was only doing her due diligence before investing in their work. Her recent obsession with similar projects had already padded her bank account quite nicely.

Ruby calculated an estimate of how much it would take to win the auction, as she'd fallen in love with the dumb animation of a cartoon zombie cat. What was the point of adult money if she couldn't spend it on shit like that? Huh?

She happened to be staring at a section of the blockchain ledger, debating her options, when it flickered. She blinked and...something changed. She hissed, "What. The. Fuck."

After scrubbing her eyes, Ruby tapped a few keys, engaging a security feature of the Shields system that archived automatic snapshots. She flung a recent screen capture up on a monitor and drew the blockchain code to the one next to it so she could compare them side by side. She wasn't losing it. They were different. The blockchain had been altered. That was...*impossible*. Or should have been.

An icy chill raced down her spine, making her sit up straight. She leaned in, her fingers tap dancing across her keyboard as she investigated. Her heart pounded harder and faster than the thumping Ace and Liam inflicted on her poor wall night after night. She wasn't sure she even remembered to breathe.

So a double tap on her shoulder shattered her concentration. The unexpected sensation would have rocketed her out of the fancy black leather gaming chair with purple trim she'd insisted their office manager, James, buy for her workstation, except she was tethered to the desk by her damn headphone cord.

Ruby screeched and jerked back, her neck contorting when the cable reached its limit.

"Sorry!" Liam hovered over her as if her earlier thoughts had conjured him. And where he was, Ace was never far behind. He sidled up beside his partner at Shields...and at home. The assessing stare from his gold eyes roved over her face, which could have probably rivaled a gallon of milk for its whiteness right then. "It's late. Everything okay?"

Ruby couldn't speak. Dizzy from the blood leaching from her cheeks and the terror coursing through her, she blinked her watery eyes furiously, then stammered, "Sure. Fine. Everything's peachy. Sorry, guys, but I need to concentrate right now."

Though she usually had a hard time peeling her hopefully not-too-blatant stare from Liam's tall, thick frame, or the tattoos winding seductively around Ace's recently healed forearm and neck, right then all she could do was gawk at the evidence in front of her.

"On what?" Liam leaned in as if anything on her screen would make sense to him. How could it when it didn't compute for her?

Ruby canted her head like a confused dog and refreshed her screen a few times but the anomaly persisted.

"I'm not sure... I was increasing my staking positions of various crypto because House of Goblins is releasing an NFT I wanted to get in on and I noticed something weird with the blockchain." She rambled mindlessly as she tried to figure out what the hell had just happened.

"What's blockchain?" Ace asked.

"It's the foundation for cryptocurrencies." She wrestled her annoyance as she filled them in on the most basic fundamentals while she tried to solve a complex problem.

"And NFT stands for...?" Liam wondered.

"Non-fungible token." Ruby spoke on autopilot as she continued to probe the faulty code and look for a way to fix it. Or uncover some clue as to who had tampered with it. She jammed her digital fingers into every nook and cranny she could find, downloading as much of her findings as possible to study later as she went. "It's digital art. Potentially very valuable if you get in early and sell to the right person."

"Damn, Ruby. You're so fucking smart, you make me feel like I've got rocks for brains." The weight of the gazes Liam and Ace were exchanging over her head pressed down on her. They probably thought she was a weirdo to be so into what she was doing. They had no idea how screwed she was and the size of the can of worms she'd inadvertently opened.

"I'm not. I'm a fucking idiot. Because while my transaction was processing, I was digging around on the creators to see what I could find out and decide if this was going to be a good investment, which is a little bit of a no-no." Ruby began to rock as she filled them in on the tiniest hint of how horribly this had just gone. It wasn't like she'd been intending to dox anyone. She was naturally curious and often poked around where...*technically*...she wasn't supposed to. While it had gotten her wrist slapped a few times, nothing awful had ever come of it. She was too damn good for that.

Except tonight, she'd met her match. And then some.

"I see." Of all the Shields, Ace would probably be the one to understand best. He had a reputation for doing some reckless shit, even on assignment. Which was probably why Liam watched him like a hawk in the field. Especially since he'd gotten hurt during the operation where Marcus and Kennedy had found Knox.

As she attempted to draw one ragged breath after another through her chattering teeth, someone took control of her computer without tripping any of her breach alerts. Her mouse moved and it wasn't because of her trembling fingers. Whoever was driving her machine began to erase screenshots even as she flew into action double checking the security of their archives and making sure the invaders couldn't move beyond her terminal to the network where duplicates had automatically been saved. It was worse than she'd imagined. *Holy shit!*

"You pissed someone off?" Liam grew more serious and crouched beside her, his concern wrapping around her like a warm blanket though it couldn't reach her core, frozen by dread. "Are you in trouble?"

"So. Much." Ruby bit her lower lip. "Look. You should go. Forget you saw me in here and that we had this conversation. This is...bad. *Really* bad."

"Like fucking hell we will." Ace balled his fists as if he could fight a virtual enemy the way he did the physical ones that often surrounded them.

"I wanted to be sure about what I was seeing before I brought this up to Jordan or JRad. It happened so fast." Ruby pinched the bridge of her nose as her security protocols seemed to engage and her mouse steadied. She'd never been so disturbed in her entire life.

"What did you uncover?" Liam wondered.

"This shouldn't be possible," Ruby muttered below her breath as she did as much damage-control as possible, disconnecting the rest of the Shields' servers and isolating her workstation from the rest of the network. Still, she couldn't help but probe deeper in case all traces of what she'd seen vanished. Which was when she realized it wasn't one independent fluke. There was a systematic change taking place across multiple blocks in the chain. "Someone is scamming the system. These aren't real sequences. It's like they're printing fake money. Billions and billions of dollars' worth. If this came out, it would undermine every cryptocurrency and the entire market could collapse. It would be a global disaster."

She'd barely choked out the confession when the hackers attacking the system breached her temporary reinforcements. They were back, taking control of her computer once more.

Ruby's spine went ramrod straight and a zing of electricity traveled through her.

An animated mask appeared across all twelve of her monitors, speaking in an eerie, distorted voice. "You're going to leave now. And consider yourself lucky that all we've taken for bothering us is your life savings. Next, we come for you. Don't think those assholes you work with can protect you either. We see everything. We know everything. And we'll be watching you even more closely now."

After displaying her crypto wallet with a zero balance, the screen went black. Her processor overclocked and acrid wisps rose from the fried equipment, threatening to set off their smoke detectors.

Ruby recoiled, drawing her feet onto the seat of her gaming chair. Unable to hold the weight of her throbbing head, her neck bowed until her forehead met her knees. She buried her face in the gap between her thighs and her chest as if that could hide the fact that she was sobbing from Liam or Ace.

"Enough!" Liam scooped her from the chair and bundled her in his mammoth arms, crushing her to his chest as if he could do one damn thing to protect her. To defend all of them, now that she'd drawn the wrath of whoever-the-fuck was powerful enough and evil enough to do what she'd witnessed.

"Where are we going?" Ace flanked them instinctively, watching their backs as Liam carried her toward the elevators.

"Upstairs. Our place." Liam barked. "Notify Jordan. Get him to lock this place down."

Ace had his phone out and was talking to their boss in a matter of moments. "We've got a problem. Code Red. Gather the team at our place. It's not safe to talk in the command center. Bring your weapons."

Ruby clutched Liam's shoulders as they rose in the elevator to their floor. She wished the ringing alarms, the slam of the metal shutters over all their exterior windows, and the unconventional army assembling in the hallways would be of any use against the kind of enemy they'd never faced before.

This time brawn wasn't going to cut it. They needed brains. And quick.

2

———

Ace had been in plenty of life-or-death situations. He'd never been as afraid as when he studied Ruby shuddering in Liam's grasp as they rushed down the corridor to their apartment across the hall from hers on the fourth floor of the Shields complex. It was pretty fucked up that even as he severed the connection with Jordan and prepared their living space to be overrun by the rest of their team, part of him was jealous as fuck that his partner got to be on comfort duty.

He'd been dying to know what it would be like to have Ruby in his arms for months. Of course, he'd prefer it to have been under far different circumstances. And hell, who knew if his bum arm would even work long enough for him to shelter the woman both he and his partner had a massive crush on?

Ace glanced over in time to watch Liam sink onto their humungous leather couch while rubbing Ruby's back and murmuring some ridiculous reassurance in her ear. Over her shoulder, he met Ace's stare, his golden gaze as disturbed as Ace was himself that they might be lying to her.

What if this mess didn't actually end up all right?

It was an epic clusterfuck he could barely comprehend, never mind fix.

Fuck. He'd spent the last several months feeling—no, *being*—completely useless as the bones in his arm knit themselves back together with assistance from an array of titanium hardware. Sidelined, he'd watched Liam charge into danger over and over, while Ace's less-toned-than-usual ass warmed a chair in the command center instead of having his partner's back.

He'd barely gotten his cast off and started regaining his strength when this happened.

Son of a bitch.

Ace didn't have long to pout before footsteps clomped down the hall from the direction of Tavish and Legend's apartment. Legend bellowed, "Yo! What the fuck is going on?"

Ace yanked open the door to admit them before they busted it down. In their place, he would have done the same. Code Red was one they'd never used before at the Shields' headquarters. An attack on their home base. It was a circumstance they'd dreaded and trained rigorously for because they, and more importantly, the loved ones of some of their teammates lived on the premises.

It was their worst nightmare that the evil bastards they stalked and eliminated could find them there. They'd practiced for all sorts of emergencies—an invasion, a siege, hell, even a bombing. But not this.

How could they fight some keyboard warrior who could be anywhere in the world and still threaten Ruby along with the rest of their team, which had become family by choice?

The duo bristled as they entered, fully prepared to kick ass. Tavish's ginger man-bun bobbed as he scanned the room. Behind him, Legend—who gave Liam a run for his money in the size department, though he was dark where Liam was light—peered over his head, relaxing when the only thing he spied was the three of them huddled together.

Ruby clung to Liam, burying her face in the crook of his neck and beefy shoulder. Ace knew what it felt like to be bundled up in all that muscle and steel even if he only experienced it during the precious moments they were fucking. With Liam's arms around her, it would be possible to imagine she was safe even though it was only an illusion. Even Liam, or Ace, or the rest of the badasses they lived and worked with wouldn't be able to stop the people coming for her now. They weren't fighting a typical war.

Her tears left a damp spot on Liam's T-shirt and she croaked, "This is mortifying."

She tried to peel herself from his hold, but he didn't budge, refusing to let her scoot away simply for the sake of her pride. Not when she needed what little comfort they could give and no one in their inner circle would blame her for taking it after she'd been so viciously attacked.

"No one here is going to judge you. Stay." Ace ran his fingers through her hair from where he stood guard beside them on the other side of the arm of the couch. He wiped tears from her silky cheek with his thumb.

"You okay, Ruby?" Tavish asked, his Scottish accent thickening as he transitioned from fight mode.

"No," Ace responded at the same time she said, "I will be. Just...shocked, I guess."

The elevator dinged in the hallway at the same time the door to the stairwell clanged. Within seconds, the available air in the room was sucked out and replaced by a horde of bristling, do-gooder assassins.

Jordan strode inside flanked by Sola, Aarav, Marcus, Kennedy, Knox, Nolan, Ransom, and Levi. The gang instinctively spread out across the open living and dining area, while covering the door and windows. Jordan turned to his soldiers and said, "James is on his way in. Someone will need to let him in the back way."

Which they all knew meant through their secret access in the basement. James—their office manager, who used to be a construction worker—had built the tunnel with assistance only from his previous and trusted crew. It connected to the cellar of their friend Devra's restaurant, a few blocks over.

"We're on it, boss." Levi jerked his chin toward the exit. Ransom pivoted on his heel before the partners had even come to a stop, off to do whatever the team needed.

"Report," Jordan ordered as he faced Ruby, his tone clipped but calm.

Ruby drew a shaky breath. She still needed a minute and Jordan wasn't about to wait. So Ace volunteered what he could. "Ruby was working on something downstairs and hackers attacked her. They fucked around with code that shouldn't have been able to be changed. And when she caught them, they came after her. It has to do with crypto. They also stole her money before threatening to do worse than just take her cash if she didn't start minding her own business. Right? Is that the gist of it?"

Ruby looked up at him as if amazed he could recap

even that much. He knew he had a habit of putting his boot in his mouth and he honestly didn't care to pay attention to most serious subjects, but when it came to her—and especially her safety—she had his full attention.

"That's a good start." Ruby nodded. She cleared her throat and scrubbed her eyes with white-knuckled fists.

Being surrounded by their friends might make her feel slightly steadier. Though only physically. The real danger here wasn't something Ace could punch or Liam could shoot.

"Thanks...for coming so fast." Ruby tried to get herself together, but her hiccups undermined her attempts at putting on a brave face.

Sola flipped her gun around and handed it safely to one of her boyfriends, Aarav. She and Kennedy were Ruby's best friends. The women approached Ruby, and Liam reluctantly loosened his arms so she could slip into the seat next to him instead of remaining curled up on his lap.

Ruby hugged Kennedy and Sola even as their medic murmured a few questions to ensure she was stable before they proceeded. It was progress.

But not enough.

"We can't really protect you. Not fully. Can we?" Ace swallowed hard and glanced at the floor. His self-esteem had taken a bigger beating than his arm when he'd been injured, and now this...right when he was about to turn things around and make his comeback.

Ruby wasn't about to lie, though. She winced and shook her head. "Not from...this."

"What *exactly* are we talking about?" Jordan asked again, less intensely this time.

"How much do you know about crypto?" Ruby wondered.

"I hear people talk about how it's bad for the environment and uses a lot of energy," Tavish responded. "Is that true?"

"Kind of. Some cryptocurrencies rely on proof of work to validate new additions to the blockchain. Basically that's a race between tons of computers to solve a problem and then tell all the other computers the solution in order to prove they did the work to find the answer. As a prize, that computer's owner gets to write the next block in the chain, which contains details about a transaction, and gets rewarded with a hefty fee. That's how things started out, anyway.

"Some of us who deal with first-generation systems buy carbon offsets to decrease the environmental impact of using so much energy and will keep doing so until that approach is entirely phased out. The future of this technology is to use staking instead. Which means, in the simplest of terms, that instead of trying to win a computer race, you're putting up some of your own money in order to volunteer to write the next block. If you were a bad actor, then you could get your stake taken away, so you have incentive to play by the rules. When we do it this way, as most systems are evolving to, there is far less energy usage. But in all cases, for blockchain to sustain itself, users have to have trust in the system, which is what these processes ensure."

"And something broke that process tonight?" Jordan's eyes narrowed as he started to catch on.

"Yes, exactly." Ruby grew more animated, her teary eyes wide and her hands flying as she nerdified them all, just a little. "Blockchain technology is a decentralized form of record keeping. It cuts out the middleman like banks or lawyers or people who traditionally held power because they maintained systems and had the final say, for example, on who owned what. Blocks are really simply ledger entries, like in accounting. It's a way to edit information like current bank balances or ownership of land without changing the historical record, which everyone can view. Theoretically, you should need control of fifty-one percent of the resources mining or staking in order to change the blockchain. On the scale we're talking about, no one person could achieve that without spending more than it would be worth to do so, so it's safe for everyone."

Jordan mulled that over while Ace's head started aching with his attempt to keep up. How the hell did someone think of all that in the first place? Their boss finally tapped his temple as what she was telling them sank in. "So you're saying you witnessed someone edit an existing block in the chain."

"It's impossible...but yes. I swear I did. And I have proof saved to our network, although I took it offline temporarily to keep it safe from the hackers." Ruby sighed. Her forehead scrunched and she shook her head, glancing up and away as if rewatching those screens in her memory. "I was poking around to see if there was any dirt on the founders of an obscure coin not worth shit, one nobody will likely realize is being tampered with either. What I saw tells me whoever these assholes are...they're testing some kind of virus that tricks the system into giving them a false majority and then hides their tracks. And it's working. They could write themselves into billions of dollars if they attacked a major currency like Bitcoin or Ethereum."

"Or take someone else's money..." Ace glared. He hadn't forgotten they'd robbed her too.

Ruby winced. "That's a separate issue. They're good. Really good. My wallet should have been secure without my key. But I verified and they weren't bluffing. It's empty."

"How much are we talking here?" Jordan asked. "What did they steal from you?"

"Around five million." Ruby's shoulders slumped.

Ace froze. "Five million coin thingies, right?"

Surely one of them wasn't that valuable. Maybe that only added up to like fifty cents, though the flush rising up her cheeks was telling him otherwise.

"No, *dollars*." Ruby rolled her eyes. "Fortunately, what they assumed was my life savings was only one of my crypto wallets. But still. Fuck them."

"Hold on." Liam looked over at Ace as if to confirm he'd heard correctly. "You're telling us you're loaded? Even aside from the ridiculous salary Jordan pays us all?"

Ruby shrugged. "Five million bucks less loaded than this morning, but I don't work here for the money. I do it because it's the right thing to do...and because it's usually fun fucking with the bad guys. Jordan promised me he'd eventually let me do that more, covering my ass while I expanded our infosecurity services into some, ahem, gray-hat realms like tracking the distributors of ransomware, subverting people selling harvested data on the dark web, developing threat intelligence and stuff like that."

Jordan beamed at her. "You do it so well. You've been there for us when we needed you to support our missions. I hope you know we're here for you until this is resolved."

Ruby relaxed then, leaning into Liam's side and

squeezing Sola's hand. "Shields are the good guys, even if we sometimes do bad things."

Ace had always known Ruby was a genius. But now he was sure of just how far beyond him she was. What the hell could someone like him have to offer her? These days it wasn't even physical protection since he'd been out of commission. Still, he'd do his best to live up to the faith Jordan was placing in each of them. If he couldn't defend her himself, he'd find out who could and convince them to come onboard.

As he usually did, Liam read his mind. He asked calmly, his voice never rising, despite the rage simmering in his gaze, "If we can't help you, who can?"

"I need JRad." Ruby squeezed her eyes shut and pressed her shaking fingers to her temples. She clearly despised asking for assistance and inconveniencing her friends as much as Ace had these past several months.

"Who's that?" Liam wondered. No one else seemed to pick up on the thread of irritation or maybe jealousy in his roommate's tone, but Ace knew the man better than anyone, maybe even than Liam knew himself.

"He's my mentor." Ruby swatted Liam's rock-solid abs with the back of her hand. Apparently she could read him pretty well too. "Officially, he's the head specialist for the OSPD cybercrimes department. But he has facets to him that are...unexpected."

"Is this the guy you told us about? The one who's a cop by day and runs a BDSM club with his wife at night?" Sola seemed to know a decent amount about the guy.

"Yeah. And that's not all he gets into. Most of the time he hands stuff off to me when it would jeopardize his job to, let's say, push the boundaries of the law. Taking him away from his wife, Lily, and their son—who, with genes from both of those two, can be a handful and a half—is the last thing I'd do if I could think of another way to handle this."

"He'll help." Jordan said simply.

"I know. That's the problem. He'd do it even if it was a massive inconvenience for his family, or the rest of the Men in Blue, needed him instead. Because he's too damn honorable not to." Ruby groaned as if that was a bad thing. Ace thought the guy sounded like someone he'd like to have on his side. Especially if the dude could help keep Ruby safe. "If it's not too much trouble, he should come in person."

"I'm sending Aven for him right now." Jordan referred to their in-house pilot. Having a private jet came in handy. "We won't use any of our external communications until the two of you can clear them as clean. Why don't you write him a quick note with the crux of the issue so he can be mulling it over on the flight here?"

"Fine." Ruby glowered.

Good. Pissed-off Ruby was way better than cowering, bawling Ruby. Seeing her as broken as Ace had often felt lately had damn near made his balls shrivel. He'd never watched her shrink from a problem, never mind shut down like that. And he never wanted to again.

"I'm sorry, Jordan." Ruby deflated. "I shouldn't have been poking around on the work computer."

He waved her off. "It's literally your job to stop shit like this. If you hadn't done it, you wouldn't have spotted these thieves, and at the end of the day, that's a bigger problem right now than even our own security or your personal finances. Besides, I'm pretty sure the only way you can get training in the services you and JRad convinced me to start offering is through *hands on* experience. You were upfront with me about that and the risks it entails."

The corner of Ruby's mouth kicked up just enough to flash the ghost of one of her adorable dimples. Ace would take that.

"We'll get to the bottom of this once JRad gets here and the two of you tell us what else you need." Jordan clapped his hands and rubbed them together. "Until then, it'd be best if you rest up and get ready for whatever's about to come. It feels like we're going to need your undivided attention if we have any chance at stopping these fuckers from causing more harm. Plus, of course, recover your savings then make sure they can never pull this shit again."

Ace cracked his knuckles. Finally, something he could be of use with. That last bit was for the rest of the Shields, he was sure of it.

Ruby struggled to her feet as if they were about to let her waltz out of there without an escort. Liam braceleted her wrist easily with his heavy hand. "Where are you going?"

"Home to cry myself to sleep, if you don't fucking mind." She sniffled but lifted her chin, some of her usual spunk returning.

"I do, actually." Liam didn't let go even when she tugged.

Ruby flung her gaze to Jordan as if demanding her boss order Liam to release her.

Ace held his breath, blowing it out only when Jordan shook his head. "It's better if you stay with Liam and Ace. First, you shouldn't be alone right now. None of us should. I'm going to ship all non-essential family members out to the Hot Rods. They can camp out in the rooms over the garage with those guys and the Powertools to help look out for them. Everyone else should be buddied up at all times. We're not going to let our guard down or make ourselves easy targets, hear me?"

A round of agreements and nods swept the room.

"Second, if whoever launched that cyberattack downstairs really did figure out who you are, they might somehow have access to your system or your room for surveillance. It's smarter for you to be where you're not usually and these two aren't nearly as connected, so it will be easier to sweep their place." Jordan crossed his arms.

"I hate it when you make sense." Ruby crashed back onto the couch dramatically, her wrist breaking free of Liam's grip, which slid to her knee instead. Ace didn't blame his partner one bit.

3

Ruby shifted, the unfamiliar sensation of something warm and smooth beneath her cheek rousing her from a fitful doze. Buttery leather creaked a bit as she resettled where she had curled up. Ah yes, on the couch in Liam and Ace's apartment. It smelled so nice, like them. She snuggled under the super-soft blanket Liam had draped over her as she had drifted off, exhausted and crashing from her adrenaline high following their team brief. Despite the perfectly toasty setting on the guys' thermostat, she hadn't been able to stop shivering. In the twilight space between sleep and wakefulness, she let her mind wander to anything but the traumatic events of the evening.

It was weird how each of the Shields had the same amount of space within the building, but the Powertools crew, led by James, had managed to create so many different layouts. On top of that, Laurel and Kate had designed a wide variety of decors to ensure each of them felt right at home. To be honest, Liam and Ace's style was the most like hers. If they'd knocked out the adjoining wall between their homes, the transition would have been pretty seamless.

There wasn't too much glass or steel like in Marcus's modern and sophisticated pad. Or the jungle of plants and bronze highlights of Aarav's. No, their place was leather and comfort. Slate grays and blues on the walls and furniture you weren't afraid to slouch on. The only difference was they didn't have nearly as many tech gadgets or elven swords lying around as she did. Her inner geek was hard to suppress.

Ruby sighed, reminding herself not to get too comfortable in their home.

Even now, she could hear them speaking, low and urgent, not quite arguing but...tense...all because of her and the shit she'd stirred up. Her stomach clenched and she gripped the throw, tuning in to what the guys were saying to distract herself from the dread that threatened to swamp her again.

"Look, Jordan was right. We should get some rest." Ace seemed to be trying to defuse Liam. He was good at knocking the serious edges off the guy with his antics, and probably with his body when no one else was around. "This JRad dude will be here in the morning and that's when this is really going to ramp up. Whatever they find, we're going to have to fix eventually, once we take this shit offline and into the real world."

Ruby hadn't thought that far ahead, but he was probably right. The Shields weren't the sort to sit by idly and allow someone to abuse the system, not when the repercussions could affect nearly every person on the planet. Whoever was doing this would have to be stopped. Not only by squashing the malignant code they had already engineered, but also by preventing them from ever creating more like it.

She blinked her eyes open and couldn't peel them away from the two men sitting across from each other at their kitchen table. Liam took up so much space, not only with his broad shoulders or the physique he worked hard on in the gym every damn day, but also with his presence. He wasn't the sort of guy who blended into the background. No, he drew attention. Especially hers. His wheat-colored beard was a shade darker than his hair, but both were groomed perfectly. They framed golden eyes flecked through with bits of russet and moss that never ceased to dazzle her in bright light.

Across from him, Ace slouched in his chair with his shirt off. Black-and-gray tattoos wound around his arm and spilled onto one side of his chest. They were only interrupted by the raw slash of pink from his fresh scar. Though he was more compact than Liam, he reminded her of some primal predator with barely enough fat padding his muscles to prove he was more than capable of fending for himself.

"I'll stay out here and watch over Ruby. You go ahead." Liam folded his hands on his stomach.

"No way. You go and *I'll* cover her," Ace argued. Knowing they had her back did far more than their blanket to warm her up from the inside out. She wished it had something to do with her personally rather than the fact that they were noble as fuck beneath Ace's ink and Liam's dense skull. "All I've been doing lately is fucking resting and I'm sick of it. You've been out there taking on the hard work while I've been sitting around with my thumb up my ass. I won't let anything happen to her."

"Ace..."

"Don't you trust me anymore?" he asked quietly, his dark scruff moving as his jaw clenched. Wrecking his arm had apparently broken a lot more than his perfect form. His confidence had shattered along with his bones. And Liam babying him because he was freaked out about almost losing the guy wasn't helping in the least.

Ruby had the urge to get up and hug them both. Instead, she cowered under her fuzzy blanket and eavesdropped, still traumatized by her earlier encounter and the lingering guilt that somehow she'd brought this massive pile of shit on them.

"Of course I do." Liam cleared his throat. "It's just that the stakes are really high. I'm as freaked out as you are that those assholes could actually find her, and I don't want anyone hurting either of you."

"Are you my partner or my dad?" Ace scoffed.

"Fuck that. You know I don't think of you like a kid, never mind my own." Liam growled, sending shivers down Ruby's spine. Fuck, that was the sexiest sound she'd ever heard in her life. It was also a warning, one Ace apparently didn't intend to heed.

"I don't know shit anymore. Everything changed the minute I got hurt on the job." Apparently Ace wasn't any clearer on their relationship status than Ruby or the rest of the Shields, though she and her friends had certainly speculated about it more than once.

"It wasn't a fucking paper cut. You took a bullet. It shattered your fucking arm. A few millimeters in another direction and it could have done a hell of a lot worse." Something—a vein, a tendon, Ruby wasn't an expert in anatomy like Kennedy—in Liam's neck bulged like it had when she'd studied it up close earlier while he'd held her.

She probably should have let her hosts know she was

awake, but who was she to interrupt what was obviously an important conversation for Ace, if not for them both? Ruby knew what it was like to doubt herself. Unlike Ace, she didn't have anyone to grab her by the throat, literally, and remind her of her value. To reinforce how much they cared.

She didn't blink one single time as Liam drew Ace to him with that huge hand on the other man's neck and crushed his mouth to Ace's. Their kiss started kind of awkwardly, Ace stiff in Liam's grasp. But it didn't take long for Liam to melt Ace's unusually prickly exterior.

Liam slid his hand up to Ace's hair, his fingers brushing over the short-cropped onyx strands and massaging Ace's scalp. Ruby imagined how good it would feel to relent and admit Liam's probing tongue between her own lips, as Ace reluctantly did.

She could see him fighting a losing war. One where he tried to hold himself separate from Liam when it was obvious he wanted nothing more than to be close to the man.

If Liam had been leveling that smoldering stare at Ruby, she wouldn't have stood a chance. She'd have flung herself at him, knocked his chair over, and still not stopped making out with him even as they crashed to the ground.

Ace emitted a sound that was half plea and half strangled resignation. Tortured and desperate, it did weird things to Ruby's insides. Made everything from her toes to the tips of her fingers tingly and restless. He wrapped his arms around Liam's shoulders and hugged him as he leaned into the exchange. Liam rewarded him by deepening their kiss, tilting his head for better access.

Ruby's eyes grew wide in the dim light as she strained

for a better view of what she'd heard so often but only imagined in the past. Liam was a rock in human form—steady, solid, unflinching. Ace was a flirt with a puppy-dog demeanor, which necessitated being bopped on the nose every once in a while. Together, they were the best of both worlds.

She wasn't sure exactly how long they went at it while she stared, transfixed by their dysfunctional beauty, but she could have watched them tasting and tempting each other for hours.

Eventually Liam leaned in and his hands dropped lower to Ace's ass. He cupped it and squeezed, lifting the guy—who was not exactly delicate himself—into his lap. Their chests pressed together and Ace's arms went immediately around Liam, his injured one on top. He ground against his partner even as Liam guided his hips.

And when Liam broke away long enough to bite Ace's lips, he groaned.

Ruby didn't mean to, but she mirrored his utterance in a much softer, reflexive echo.

The men froze, then broke apart.

Ace scrambled off Liam so fast he would have crashed to the floor if Liam hadn't had his hands still in the vicinity of Ace's trim waist to steady him.

"We can't do this. Not with *her* here," Liam whisper-shouted to Ace.

Ace went still and deflated like one of those wobbly signs in front of a car dealership when the wind died. Was Liam ashamed of what they did together? Was that why they kept things strictly behind closed doors...? Well, up against the wall between their apartments. Or were they granting her some sort of professional courtesy?

If it was the latter, Ruby would have assured them she didn't mind their show in the least.

"I need to hit the shower before bed." Liam's voice was rough as he ran his hands through his hair. Even his brisk rubs couldn't entirely put the medium-length top, which faded into shaved sides, back in order after Ace had mauled it. His gilt hair twinkled in the glow from the under-cabinet lights in the kitchen beyond. Sure, they'd been sparring in the gym before they'd found her in crisis earlier, but Ruby would bet money Liam's primary objective had more to do with his impressive hard-on than cleaning himself. That massive bulge in his shorts *had* to ache.

"Go ahead." Ace nodded. "I can hold down the fort for ten minutes."

"Of course you can." Liam didn't argue. "When I'm done, I'm going to crash. Alone. In my room. Work out the rest with our guest, huh? It'd be better if you let her have your bed, so there's another layer of insulation between her and the front door or the windows." Liam attempted a smile, but it was nearly as strained as his voice...and his shorts.

Ruby wondered if they were embarrassed by what they shared. She sure as fuck wasn't. It was something darker that washed over her as she replayed their kiss in her head for what she was sure would be the first of a million times.

Ruby tried not to let the swirls of envy erase her genuine happiness for the guys. No matter what Sola, Kennedy, and Laurel kept telling her, these two didn't need—or want—anyone else. Those sparks of attraction she'd imagined she'd felt from time to time were nothing compared to the blaze they'd ignited in each other moments earlier. After seeing firsthand the passion between them, Ruby was certain they were enough for each other.

So why did they seem so twisted up about it? And why weren't they more open with the team about their relationship? It wasn't like anyone kept their private life to themselves around the place.

Hell, half the times she went to use the pool or hot tub or steam room she waltzed in on some porn-worthy activities. Kennedy, Sola, and Laurel were constantly comparing notes on their newfound threesomes and James—well, shit—that man had stories about orgies with his old Powertools crew and their wives that she wouldn't believe if they'd come from anyone else. Even Jordan had been known to take a break from boss-man mode when his wife Wren and husband Kason were around.

Ruby let her eyes close again as she wondered if she'd ever find someone who looked at her like the people she was surrounded with daily looked at their lovers.

"Hey." Ace startled her when he cupped her shoulder and shook her gently. "Sorry to wake you, but Liam and I think it's best if you sleep in my room."

"Oh. Uh, 'kay." She didn't have to fake the rasp in her voice. Except it came from being turned on, not being asleep. Before she could untangle herself from the blanket, Ace's arms scooped her up from the couch and cradled her against his chest. "So different."

"Huh?" he wondered as he carried her effortlessly to his room. Her mind went wild imagining it was for far different reasons.

"Than Liam." She nuzzled her face against his neck shamelessly, hoping to dull some of the sting of his roommate's rejection.

"Oh, yeah. I'm bony and scrawny compared to him."

She laughed. "Not how I would have described you. Am I hurting your arm?"

"It's fine." He didn't answer her directly, nor did he set her down until it was on top of his mattress, which put the couch to shame in the comfort category. She felt like she was nestling into a cloud and she never wanted to leave.

Ruby stretched like a cat, rubbing herself on every bit of his bedding in the process. Oops.

"You want me to run over to your place and get you some stuff?" Ace asked. "I mean, not that pajamas are required here, feel free to sleep naked if that's your thing, but I'll go get them if you want."

Ruby laughed. As if she'd strip down in front of these two and their bazillion abs. "Thanks. I usually sleep in only a T-shirt, so this is fine, but my toothbrush would be great, and, uh…"

"What?" He dusted a stray hair from her face.

"My emoji pillow and stuffies. I can't sleep without them." She figured her cheeks were as red as her hair at that point, but really, was it any surprise to them that she was a massive dork? "The poop one seems especially appropriate tonight."

He laughed. "You got it. I'll be right back. Make yourself comfortable…in my bed, I mean."

"Are you sure this is okay?" Ruby double-checked, not because she didn't want to burrow into his pillows and fall asleep surrounded by that leather-and-spice smell that had lulled her earlier, but because he had to be ragged inside still from Liam shoving him away so fast.

"Yeah, of course." He nodded. "Liam called it. It's best if there's another barrier between you and any access into the building. Feel free to lock yourself in even."

"You're not planning on joining me?"

"In bed?" Ace's brows climbed his forehead.

"I mean, your couch is comfortable, but it's not going to be big enough for you to stretch out on, is it?"

"I'll make it work." Ace shrugged.

"Don't be dumb. We're adults. And cramming your arm into weird positions all night isn't going to feel great. Unless...sleeping next to me makes you uncomfortable."

Ace snorted, then mumbled something under his breath that sounded like, "Only in the best of ways. No worse than Liam leaving me hanging."

"What was that?" Ruby's eyes narrowed. Surely she could not have heard him right.

"I said I'll be right back with your stuffed shit. Not that I'm criticizing you. I meant that literally." Before she could call him on that obvious lie, he'd left the apartment. The keypad outside beeped as he activated their alarm.

Ruby had slipped out of her jeans and was still wide awake, wearing her T-shirt and panties, staring at the ceiling of Ace's room from his huge bed, when the other side dipped. She closed her eyes, unwilling to argue or ruin this chance to sleep next to one of the very few people who could make her feel safe given the circumstances. Ace melted her heart a little as he set up a wall between them, using her stuffed animals as a fluff-filled barrier. Whether it was to make her feel secure, or to keep either of them from crossing into awkward territory during the night, she had no idea.

She wondered why Liam and Ace slept in separate beds—in different rooms, even—when she knew damn well they were intimate. Were they only fuck buddies and not more?

Did either of them realize how much they were

missing out on by denying the powerful connection between them and reducing it to merely something physical when clearly, for Ace at least, it ran far deeper than their dicks.

They were as fucked up as she was. And somehow that made her feel better. Enough that her eyes closed and her breathing evened out. She verged on falling into true slumber.

"Sleep well, Ruby," Ace whispered into the darkness, though he had no idea she could hear him. "I promise I won't let anyone hurt you. Not even me or Liam. He's right. It's better not to drag you into our mess."

4

Liam didn't feel the least bit bad for Ace when he stifled another yawn behind his fist. It was his own damn fault he hadn't slept the night before, probably spending every instant memorizing the view of Ruby in his bed. In his place, Liam would have done exactly the same thing, especially knowing there were assholes out there who wanted to attack her.

They'd have to come through him, and Ace, first.

Speaking of their badass computer nerd, she was contorted into the sleek black-and-purple seat James had brought up from the command center for her. He swore the woman violated every ergonomic principle ever created, resembling a pretzel more than a person with one foot tucked under her and the other thigh draped over her bent knee. An elbow propped on her stacked legs made a stand for her to hold her chin as she studied a bunch of gobbledygook on a monitor James had delivered along with the chair. Apparently she was working on a local system only, analyzing the data she'd downloaded right before things had gotten hairy the night before.

"How the hell is that comfortable?" Ace asked, as if he could read Liam's mind.

"You got me." Liam shrugged. "But it's weirdly hot."

Ace huffed out a laugh. "You're telling my boner. Our job has never been so sexy before."

"We can't afford to be distracted on this one." Liam frowned. He was reminding himself more than anything, but Ace cursed as if Liam had punched him in the gut.

"You think I don't know that? Or that I'd let my libido put her in danger? If my attraction was a problem, I'd ask Jordan for a replacement myself."

Figured. Because Ace was much more honest and open about his feelings than Liam had ever managed to be. His partner would blurt them out, consequences be damned. That was something Liam had never figured out how to do. It seemed reckless. Like Ace could sometimes be.

It was one of the reasons he worried so much about the guy when they were on assignment. Exactly like he had the day he'd been injured during the ambush on Knox and Kennedy, he'd willingly throw himself in front of a bullet for someone without second thought.

That moment still haunted Liam's nightmares and likely would for life. They'd gotten so damn lucky, not that Ace would see it that way after months of recuperation.

Ruby lifted her head then and rocked it from side to side, an ominous crack emanating from her neck as she did.

"Damn, Ruby." Ace wandered over to her and laid his hands on her shoulders as if it was the most natural thing in the world. "You're tense."

She snorted at that. "Just a little."

Liam watched as the guy he fucked started massaging

the woman he wished he fucked and figured he must have done something horrific in a previous life to warrant being tortured by a double temptation so damn potent. Ace pressed his thumbs on either side of her spine, then dragged them upward along the column of her neck, which was revealed since her long, extra-vibrant red hair had been twisted and draped onto her chest.

Instead of swatting him away, Ruby sighed and released a low moan, then leaned into his touch. She accepted what little relief Ace could give. Liam tried not to be jealous, but it was no use. He should have thought of that, if he'd dreamed in a million years she'd accept that kind of comfort from him. Truth was, she might not. Ace had a natural way of putting people at ease where Liam made them nervous. That bastard.

Ace kept rubbing her porcelain skin before tossing a wink over his shoulder in Liam's direction. Liam's cock thickened, threatening to go fully hard despite the fact that he was technically on duty and any of their teammates were likely to show up to check on them or bring developments to their attention at any moment.

As Ace kept massaging, his motions grew a bit jerky in his right hand, which soon stopped moving entirely. *Shit.* Liam strode over and stood behind him, working Ace's arm, even as Ace did his best for Ruby with his left hand.

At first, Ace went stiff, resisting Liam's attention, but it was either let him do it or stop taking care of Ruby. Ace huffed then gave in, allowing Liam to comfort him as he'd wanted to so many times lately. They were one fucked-up trio.

This assignment was going to kill him.

Maybe it was time for another shower and the jerk-off session that went with it.

Before Liam could make some lame excuse and disappear under the spray for some respite of his own, a rap on the door reverberated through the room. The three of them paused, then the guys stood up straighter. Liam put his hand on his gun in its shoulder holster. Not that he truly believed the Shields' headquarters could be breached without tripping an alarm, or that an enemy would knock, but he wasn't taking chances either. "Who is it?"

"James. And I've got our visitors. Let us in."

Ruby spun in her seat so fast she nearly whacked Ace in the balls with the arm of her chair. Liam chuckled as she flew past him and ripped open the door. "JRad. Thank you for coming. I'm so sorry for dragging you away from home and your family."

A tall, deceptively strong guy—not too bulky but cut as hell, with a five o'clock shadow even before lunch—opened his arms and caught Ruby as she flung herself at him.

If Liam had been envious of Ace a minute ago, the green-eyed monster roaring to life inside him then reached legendary status. The guy held her tight without so much as a wobble when she wrapped her legs around him and went full koala. "No problem, kid. Lily says hi. And frankly, I could use a break from the little man every once in a while. He's...adorable and far too good at finding trouble to get into."

"Yeah, well, he is your son." Ruby unwound herself and JRad set her down as James looked between the pair and Liam and Ace, a stupid grin plastered on his face. What was so funny?

Liam for one found nothing about this situation amusing. Ace came to stand beside him, arms crossed, feet spread. He grumbled so only Liam could hear, "I hate him already."

JRad didn't waste time on pleasantries, though. He clearly was a cop, with an edge Liam hadn't expected. "Ruby, your note was...alarming."

"Yeah. I fucked up."

"Did you really?" JRad focused on her, making her shift. Even Liam felt the waves of intensity radiating off of the dude. They belied his geek vibes. There was far more to him than it appeared. "To me it sounds like you scored big, discovering a huge vulnerability before someone had a chance to truly exploit it fully."

"Oh. I guess. But they smashed through my security measures like they were nothing and it sounded like they figured out who I was, which shouldn't be possible. Plus they hacked one of my crypto wallets."

"They sound like a real problem."

"Thank God you're here now to fix this."

JRad took Ruby by the shoulders and stared into her gaze unflinchingly. "I'm not here to save you. You don't need me for that. I'm here to support you. And to remind you that you know what you're fucking doing. You had the best teacher, after all. So show me what you're working on and tell me what I can do to help. You're the warrior. I'm your weapon."

"Maybe he's not the actual worst," Liam grudgingly grumbled to Ace.

JRad turned to the guy behind him then. "Ruby, you remember Lucas."

"Hey." She smiled and waved at the guy a bit awkwardly. Liam didn't blame her. He didn't seem exactly like the huggable sort. Ruby backed up a bit, inviting James, JRad, and Lucas inside. "Let me gather up my equipment and we can move downstairs to the command center. There's more room there for everyone to work. You're right. We're going to take our system back and make sure those fuckers can't get in again without some nasty surprises of our own. Then *we're* going to go after *them*."

"That's what I like to hear." JRad ruffled Ruby's hair, making her smile for the first time since she'd been attacked.

While she and James started gathering her stuff, JRad and Lucas ambled over to Liam and Ace, each with an arm outstretched. As much as Liam wished he didn't have to shake, he put his hand out with respect for someone who would drop everything at a moment's notice and come to help one of their teammates.

JRad grinned as he practically crushed Liam's hand in an unexpectedly strong grip. When he spied the hellish scar on Ace's arm, he eased up a bit on the pressure but instead leaned in and said quietly, "You can chill out, guys. I'm not a threat to you. My wife would cut my dick off if I so much as looked at another woman like you're imagining."

James peeked over, witnessing their interaction. His eyes twinkled as he assessed their exchange.

Lucas laughed. "You wouldn't be so lucky, dude. Lily knows far more inventive ways to torture a man than to let you off so easily."

"Is she on the force too?" Ace asked. "Why would a cop know that?"

"Uh, no." JRad's wicked smile only spurred Liam's curiosity. "She has more specialized experience."

It was right about then that Liam remembered

someone had said JRad and his wife owned a BDSM club. *Ohhhhhh.*

Ace wasn't done digging himself a hole with his big mouth, as usual. "Ah, right. I, uh, just assumed..."

"What, that I'm the top? Well, that's dumb, but you were right." JRad was enjoying their discomfort a little too much, as was Lucas, who could barely hold back his chortles.

"But your wife..."

"She's a switch." JRad turned possessive, finally showing a glimpse of the Dom beneath the nerd. "But only for me. Everyone else...well, she'd really enjoy teaching your fine asses some manners."

Ace blinked as if imagining what it would be like to try out kneeling for a woman like that. Liam knew he would enjoy it, since Ace did it often enough for Liam and got off hard. Well, that's not where he'd expected this introduction to go. He cleared his throat. "Anyway, thanks. For coming and for...that info."

JRad lost every hint of civility and mirth when he leaned in. "For the record, Lily would do far worse to you if you don't treat Ruby right. And I would let her. We both love that girl."

"Understood." Liam nodded once. He had no intention of acting on the strange zing that passed between him and Ace whenever she was around even if it seemed she amplified whatever ill-advised attraction he and his roommate shared. That was problematic enough without involving Ruby or anyone else in their mess.

"But *you* are a cop?" Ace asked Lucas.

"Nah. I used to be an agent for a department that supposedly doesn't exist. That's how I met Jordan. But after I lost my leg during a classified op, I was no longer needed, and now I take on private odd jobs from time to time. Like this one."

Ace's eyes went wide and though he obviously tried not to stare, his gaze flicked toward the floor as if he could peek through the guy's jeans. There hadn't been any hint the man had a disability. Liam understood his partner wasn't being an insensitive asshole. It had been his worst fear that his own injury could end his career, and nearly had. Even now, they were working hard to get him up to full speed for the field.

Lucas seemed to understand. After all, there was no hiding Ace's gnarly scar. "You get hurt at work, too?"

Ace nodded, his eyes scrunching shut for a moment. "What was it like the first time you went back out? On assignment, I mean."

"Rough. Not going to lie. You're not the same person you were before. You have to learn to adapt." Lucas paused, then said, "You started practicing shooting with the other hand yet?"

Ace shook his head. "Trying to rehab the busted arm."

"Better to hone your strengths than to try to pretend like you don't have a weakness." Lucas's stare was kind.

"We have a range in the basement." Ace looked to Liam and then over at Ruby. "Maybe if they don't need us for a bit, we could get in some practice sometime."

"Sure, that sounds good." Lucas nodded.

Ace surprised Liam by turning and wandering away with Lucas instead of hanging with him and JRad. As they started to talk privately, he thought he heard Ace say, "Nah. Nothing like that. I'm too dumb for her and too weak for him. Especially now."

Liam's guts clenched. He was going to have to talk to his partner soon. But every time he tried, it ended up like the night before had. With his tongue down Ace's throat and his hands on his ass. It was much easier to fuck than to talk.

"Looks like you've gotten yourself in one hell of a tough spot here." JRad clapped Liam on the shoulder. "Don't worry. We'll figure it out."

Liam wondered what it would be like to be JRad or Lucas, so in control of his own life and at peace with himself. If JRad could help him figure this shit out, he would listen. "I'm open to advice."

"That's a great place to start." JRad smiled. "Come on, let's help Ruby and James carry this shit."

Liam nodded and got to work. At least that was easy.

5

By that evening, the situation had evolved. Ace rested his hip against the boardroom table as he and Liam took their shift guarding the nerds while they worked. The brainiacs were too engrossed in ones and zeros to have any idea if someone was sneaking up on their bodies while their minds were elsewhere.

Lucas joined them. They'd taken that trip to the range together earlier while Tavish and Legend had been on watch. The guy was pretty cool, and completely badass. If Lucas hadn't called attention to his missing limb, Ace might never have noticed. He wanted that for his arm. And after working with Lucas for a bit, he thought he had a better idea of how to move forward. Without constantly trying to recreate the way he'd been before, but by learning to leverage his advantages and avoid putting himself in a position where he had to rely on his vulnerabilities.

Ruby and JRad had been occupied non-stop for the past sixteen hours. Hardly blinking as their fingers flew over their keyboards, tossing out ideas so the other could encourage them or shoot them down. They were a dream duo in their field. Ace was sure that if he understood even a fraction of what they were up to, he'd have been hella impressed. Together, they'd secured and stress tested the Shields network. Plus JRad confirmed what Ruby had suspected.

It was good news and bad.

The actions she'd taken to boot the hackers had held. Even once they restored everything, the system withstood the attacks they could see being launched from the outside. Unfortunately, that didn't solve the bigger problem.

Someone had figured out how to alter that block stuff and was going to use that knowledge to fuck over tons of hobby investors who would have no way to fight back, worldwide. Ace intended to leave the details to the experts, but even he could see how the repercussions would ripple outward, undermining the larger ecosystem and introducing the kind of instability assholes preyed on. Technology like that would be worth a hell of a lot to the wrong sorts of buyers.

This was the kind of shit that got people killed in a hurry. If the world was lucky, the Shields would be the ones who'd pull the plug on the hackers instead of the other way around.

For the moment, Jordan had deemed the immediate physical threat to have passed. He'd brought their families home, including his own husband and wife, Kason and Wren. Not like they'd have stayed away too much longer anyway. The bonds between the people here were tight. As happy as Ace was for them, it twisted the knife in his gut to be surrounded by so many lovesick fools in healthy, blissful, committed relationships when the man he'd been obsessed with for years kept their connection a dirty secret, maybe even from himself.

Liam only admitted they were more than best friends or field partners when his dick needed sucking or a hot hole to fuck. Yet Ace didn't seem capable of saying no, not when that was what he wanted too—plus a whole lot more.

He must have shot Liam a dirty look without intending it.

"What?" the guy asked.

"Nothing." Ace shrugged. He wasn't about to get into their dysfunction there and then. It would probably lead to one of the inconsequential brawls that occasionally broke out around the place. They were men, and women, of action. Sometimes frustrations spilled over to sparring matches in the gym or tussles in the lounge, though that was a sure way to piss James off when they messed the place up.

"He's probably hangry." Lucas checked his watch. "It's been a long time since lunch and it takes a lot of energy to heal bones and rebuild muscle."

Jordan roused Ace from his dark thoughts and the denial he was about to make that he needed anything more or different than Liam when their boss joined them, his infamous Bluetooth earpiece still in place. He'd been hunkered down in his office making calls to the contacts in his intel network non-stop in an effort to pick up on any rumors floating around in the dark, sludgy underbelly of the world.

James wasn't far behind. He made their lives easier however he could. He kept things running, organized their chaos, and honed them into the sharpest spearhead they could be for Jordan. He swept his gaze around the room and asked, "Anyone need anything?"

"We need to talk. Come on, you two. You need a break anyway." Jordan might as well have been talking to the wall. Ruby and JRad kept tip-tapping away, their headsets insulating them to anything outside their bubble.

James slipped on matching gear and pressed the button on the ear. "Earth to sexy geeks. Earth to sexy geeks."

Ruby instantly spun her chair around, her eyes wide as they surveilled the room with panicky sweeps. She even untangled her legs and put her feet flat on the floor as if ready to make a run for it. Until her gaze landed on Ace's. He smiled slowly at her, hoping it reassured her that no one was about to eat her—unless it was him, and he'd make sure she enjoyed it if he was ever so lucky. She'd been jumpy as fuck since the night before and he didn't blame her one bit. Maybe he should go get one of her stuffies and set it on the desk beside her next time someone else was on official duty.

JRad rubbed his temples but shot James a wan smile. "Yeah?"

"You skipped lunch and it's already getting late. Jordan also needs to speak with the team." James pointed in the direction of the dining area across the hall, where the din of clinking silverware and conversation meant the majority of their friends and family were already gathered for a meal. "So we're going to take twenty and move this party to the kitchen unless you tell me there's something that will fall apart before we can stuff our faces. Devra catered an entire fucking buffet for us and Morgan added five dozen pastries from her shop. Let's eat."

Ace's stomach growled at the thought alone. The

women were killing it in Middletown, with lines often out the door daily, and he was one of their best customers. Between the Shields, the Powertools crews, and the Hot Rods and Hot Rides mechanic gangs, they already had an army to feed.

"You know that tunnel was intended to be a top-secret escape route, not an express lane for food delivery service. Right?" Jordan shook his head at James. Still, when the seven of them crossed the lobby and wandered into the bright and homey cafeteria, he was the first one in line to grab a plate from the stack on the expansive white marble island.

"No reason it can't be multifunctional." James shrugged. "Besides, the construction on the alternate route, beneath Blakely's future tattoo shop, is almost finished."

"Good. I like having a backup plan for our backup plans." Jordan piled some roasted vegetables and that awesome chicken in smoky, spicy sauce from their featured dish onto his plate. Despite the weight on his shoulders, he smiled when he caught Wren's gaze from across the room. Kason sat beside her, refilling her glass from a water pitcher in the center of the long community table. Then he refocused on Ruby and JRad, frowning. "Sometimes you need them. For example..."

"Oh no." Ruby's plate clattered to the counter. She snatched it up again, but Ace could see her fingers trembling. He put his hand on her shoulder and squeezed even as Liam edged closer to her other side. "What now?"

"How bad would it be, if say..." Jordan collected silverware wrapped in a napkin, then settled onto the long bench across from Wren and Kason. He forked some of his dinner into his mouth and the rest of them joined him as they finished doling out their dinners. When he continued, he had the attention of everyone in the room, their sidebar conversations hushed. "...there had been an uptick in ransomware attacks on financial institutions in the past twenty-four hours. With threats claiming to be able to wipe out and re-write transaction ledgers at will."

"*Real* bad." Ruby scrunched her eyes closed and Ace grabbed her now full plate before it could slip from her hand again, this time spilling her food everywhere.

"Take a seat." Liam cupped her elbow and escorted her to the table where Ace placed her plate in front of her and asked, "Can I get you something to drink?"

She shook her head. "I don't think I can eat. I feel sick."

"You have to keep up your strength in order to fight this to the best of your awesome abilities." Ace untangled her gorgeous mane of fiery locks and laid her hair neatly down the center of her back, which seemed to relax some of the tension in her shoulders. "You've got this."

She looked over to JRad, who nodded. "You're making progress on following the traces they left behind yesterday. You'll get them. If they had all the bugs worked out, they wouldn't be firing warning shots. They're trying to take the easy way out and get paid before they have the code locked down because they know you're on to them."

"I'd be afraid of you too if you weren't on our team," Legend said around a mouthful of buttered fresh bread. Tavish grinned from beside him, nodding as Sola and Kennedy concurred.

"Guys, they have it. It's only a matter of time before they perfect it." Ruby groaned. "No wonder they'd been testing on some random, throwaway coin. It's not only crypto they're targeting, but the entire financial sector."

JRad stabbed one of the morsels on his plate far harder than necessary. "How much are they asking for from the big banks?"

"Billions, in total." Jordan relayed the figure as if it wasn't shocking. Maybe he'd already thought this through to the end game whereas Ace had still been worrying about the immediate details, like protecting Ruby and his disastrous love life. There was a reason he wasn't in charge and he was fine with that.

"They're not going to pay it, are they?" Ruby had gone pale again. "It's a bluff! At least for the moment."

"Several key board members, CEOs, and regulatory officials led by one prominent financial guru, seem to think it will cause less damage to make this go away by any means necessary as opposed to letting even a single hint of the possibility of a hijack leak to the market. It could cause a crash the likes of which we've never seen or could recover from in the global economy." Jordan shoved his own plate away with a bit of food left on it.

That was a first.

Kason leaned over and squeezed his husband's thigh. Laurel and Jace looked to Nolan, as if trying to read how screwed they were from his expression. It was equally grim as everyone else's. *Shit. Fuck. Damn.*

Aarav set his fork down with a clink. Both he and Cash edged closer to Sola, who was sandwiched between them. Even she frowned. Marcus, Kennedy, and Knox weren't any more chipper.

"How much time do you think we have until they cave to the hackers' demands on his advice alone?" JRad asked.

Jordan wiped his mouth, then too carefully set his napkin on his abandoned plate. "A few days. Maybe a week unless someone gives them absolute assurance it's not a credible threat."

"And the reward for preventing a catastrophe like that?" Tavish wondered. As opposed to everyone else, he had no trouble packing away the delicious meal. He was cool, confident, and a little scary. Ace didn't have a problem admitting he had a bit of a work-crush on the guy.

"Negotiated at base thirty-percent of ransom avoided plus hefty incentive pay based on time to completion." Jordan looked around the table, starting with Ruby and JRad.

James stared back, his jaw slack.

"Gross, dude, no one wants to see that." Liam knocked into James, making him sway as he finished swallowing his bite.

"You might suck at math, Captain Brawny, but I don't. Construction workers use it almost as much as computer whizzes." He flicked his gaze to Ruby, then back to Jordan. "That's gonna make for a hefty Christmas bonus 'round here, boss."

The Shields shared in the profits of the enterprise. Jordan was far more generous than he needed to be. Hell, most of them would have fucked with these criminals simply because they could.

Jordan nodded. "No one here would ever have to take another assignment if they didn't want to."

"No pressure." Ruby's chin dropped to her chest, which rose and fell in an unnatural cadence as she took measured breaths.

Ace twisted so he could sling his good arm around her, tucking her tight to his side. She shot him an appreciative look through her full lashes instead of shrugging him off. So he kept it there.

Cash cleared his throat, then spoke up. "Is Albert Suisse your financial guru leading this charge?"

"Theoretically, if he was, do you have an in with him?" Jordan winged his stare to Sola and Aarav's playboy-turned-house-boyfriend.

"Yeah. One of those bullshit positions my dad set me up in when he framed me was on the board of some company Albert annexed. And although he was a total creep and far too ambitious for me to care to hang out with often, he was into yachts. Plus we're about the same age. Suisse is a legend in the industry, a self-made prodigy turned billionaire by the time he was twenty and he's not too much older now despite how influential he is. So we at least had a couple tiny things in common, which was more than I could say for most of the other assholes there. I would be happy to put in a good word for the Shields if it could buy you some more time." Cash was already taking his cell phone from the pocket of his skinny jeans.

"Okay, great." Jordan nodded. "I'd appreciate it if you did, but not on your personal phone. Use one of the ones Ruby set up to ensure a private connection."

"Ah, yeah. Sure." Cash winced as he set his cell on the table. "I forget about all this spy stuff."

"I don't." Legend leaned forward so he could claim Jordan's attention. "This is a two-pronged attack, isn't it?"

Their boss folded his hands in his lap. "Maybe. So far our contract with the bankers only covers the neutralization and elimination of the code. In my opinion, we won't know for sure this issue is resolved permanently unless we find the people who are behind it and make sure they can't do it again. We don't have authorization for that phase of the operation from the authorities...yet."

"That's fine. Because I still haven't found out more about their identities than their online aliases." Ruby sighed. "I'm working on it."

"I know you are." Jordan shot her a grim smile. "I couldn't have asked for a better lead on this project. You'll get them."

The silence lingered until James stood and started fussing...probably to take their minds off heavier topics. He went to toss his napkin and it tumbled off the heap to the floor. "Look at this pile of crap! Did no one teach you how to clean up after yourselves?"

He waved toward the overflowing garbage. His sister, Laurel, shot him a wry grin that made Ace pretty sure she had similarly lectured James when he'd been a kid.

James grumbled, "Someone better take the damn trash out."

"I thought you were obsessed with being our Alfred," Ace teased, just to rile him. He should probably stop doing immature shit like that—antagonizing the people he cared for most. It drove Liam nuts, but it was too fun not to instigate every once in a while.

"Ace. Get it straight. I always wanted to be Robin. The cute sidekick with bright, bulge-enhancing costumes. Besides, Alfred was a butler, not a maid. And I'm neither."

It was worth James's crossed arms when Ace got a glimpse of Ruby's smirk. At least she thought he was funny.

Hiding his own chuckle behind his hand, Ace soothed James's ruffled feathers by doing as asked and emptying the too-full can. With a glance at Lucas, he hefted the bulging industrial-sized sac with his left hand. It felt weird, but Lucas was correct. It would be easier to learn to do more with his good side than to constantly be stressed about whether his bum arm would hold or give out at the worst possible instant. He could get stronger like this if he worked at it, even if it was from simple shit like garbage duty.

When he kicked open the back door, someone scurried away from the steel as it swung outward.

"Son of a bitch, Ace!" Eli stumbled backward.

"Sorry, bud." Ace chucked the thick black bag into the dumpster. He didn't mean to be a loose cannon, but it seemed he came by it naturally. He caught and held the swinging door for the head Hot Rods mechanic, who was a cousin of Joe from James's original Powertools crew.

Everyone knew everyone around Middletown. It was nice to be surrounded by friends.

"What can we do for you?" Ace asked right before he noticed the neon flash of James's ever-more-ridiculous car, glowing in the lot beyond. He couldn't wait for everyone else to get an eyeful of what he was seeing. Ace leaned into the doorway and shouted, "James! Everyone! Come quick!"

Of course that lead to a damn near stampede of spies with hands inconspicuously on their various weapons as they poured from the building. They knew it wasn't dangerous or he would have given them a heads up but still, everyone was rightfully on edge and, frankly, never entirely trusting.

It was a hazard of their profession.

Ace braced his hands on his knees and bent over laughing hysterically. It felt good to shake off some of the tension that had been stalking them at work, and at home now that he and Liam had to watch themselves and Ruby was thrown into the middle of their bullshit.

"What the fuck is *that*?" Tavish pointed at the tiny car, which was overwhelmed by armored sides, bulletproof glass, and now a ten-foot-tall snorkel. Given Tavish's thick brogue, ginger coloring, and his insistence on wearing a modern black kilt with combat boots, it had to be both impressive and outlandish to make him feel it stood out.

And he was right.

Eli disguised a chuckle with a cough, then said, "James's car is even more badass than before. It's waterproof and can drive through your pond back here if he feels like it."

It looked like one of those poisonous beetles found in the jungle, tiny but dazzlingly bright to warn would-be predators to stay away. And yet, Ace had the feeling the thing was cursed. After being backed into, having a tree fall on it, and then rolling into their pond...yeah, it didn't have a great track record.

James stood straight and held out his hands for the keys. "Perfect. Thanks, Eli!"

He acted like the guy had added something practical like a set of snow tires in winter instead of...that. Lucas and JRad exchanged a perplexed stare while the rest of Shields took bets on how long it would be before some other catastrophe threatened James's pride and joy.

Still cracking up, they headed back inside together, Jordan triple-checking the exit was secured and the alarm reset while the team congregated in the lobby, making plans for evening workouts, movie screenings, or coordinating the overnight shifts.

"Hey, Wren, didn't you say you had something to tell

everyone?" Kennedy asked as the Shields got ready to disperse.

"Nah." Wren leaned up against Kason's side. He automatically wrapped his arm around her waist as she smiled over at their husband Jordan. "It's not the right time with this stuff going on. It can wait."

"In that case, I'm going to take these two for a dip in the hot tub." Kennedy motioned toward Marcus and Knox.

"A skinny dip?" Legend asked with a wry grin. "Tavish and I will be sure to go upstairs to shower instead of interrupting you after we're done lifting."

"Probably for the best." Knox took his lovers' hands and led them down the hall toward the pool and locker rooms off the gym.

"Call me if you need me. Otherwise, take care of yourself," Sola murmured to Ruby before hugging her goodnight. "And let them do that too."

Ace appreciated the good word and that Ruby's closest friends seemed to understand that he and Liam would do whatever they could to help her.

Soon enough, Ace trailed Ruby toward the command center with Liam by his side. They might as well have been her shadow and he didn't mind one bit. He'd be happy to tail her, even after this assignment was wrapped. He only hoped they were bringing her even a bit of comfort, knowing she could count on them to protect her body, if not her finances.

"Okay." Ruby cracked her knuckles as she contorted herself into her chair again. "Priorities are deconstructing the change subroutine to come up with a patch, then tracing the packet trail to identify the physical location of machines used to launch the cyberattack."

JRad shook his head. "My most urgent need is some sleep. I can't be of use to you if I'm not fresh. So I have to admit that now that I'm stuffed, I'm used up. I'm going to take a nap."

"Why do I feel like this is a trap?" Ruby narrowed her eyes at her mentor.

"Because in four hours, when I get back, you're going to debrief me on the progress you've made and the revised priority list. Liam here is going to ignore your protests and take you upstairs to put you to bed. Over his shoulder if necessary. And once you're there, Ace is going to do whatever it takes—including tying you up—to get you to stay in his bed."

Ruby glared at JRad. "Traitor."

"I only want what's best for you, kid."

"You mean rest?" Liam asked. "She can't keep doing that level of work if she can't see straight."

"Yeah. Rest. And whatever else she's been denying herself that might help her to relax some." JRad didn't budge when Ruby looked as if she might stab him with one of the jeweled dagger letter openers in the Lord of the Rings mug turned pen holder on her desk. "Don't make me call Lily. You know how intuitive she is. Not to mention unafraid of sharing her opinion when it comes to her friends' wellbeing. I'm sure she'd have a lot more to say about whatever is going on here than I just did."

JRad crossed his arms, the silver rivets on the leather cuff hugging one of them glinting in the can lighting from overhead. It wasn't a suggestion. It was an order.

Ace grinned. "He's not only smart, he's fucking brilliant. Listen to the man."

Before he could fully process the impact JRad's suggestions had on Liam, his partner leaned down and laid his palms flat on the desk, trapping Ruby so he could stare directly into her eyes. Without asking, he said, "I'm setting a timer. Not a minute beyond four hours. Be ready."

Ruby swallowed hard, but nodded.

Ace thought it might take the entire remainder of the shift before his dick would allow him to face them without making a scene, so he quickly dove into a seat at the boardroom table and tucked beneath it, prepared to keep watch from that outpost.

He'd only ever heard Liam use that tone with him before, and in private, but Ruby seemed to respond to it every bit as eagerly as Ace did.

Holy fucking shit.

JRad looked between Ace, Liam, and Ruby. He nodded once, then ambled out of the command center, whistling like he hadn't completely rewritten the rules of the game they'd been playing for months.

6

Ruby frantically entered different commands, but the hackers kept slashing through her code and getting closer to finding her. Not only in their digital arena, but at Shields. That creepy mask they'd popped on screen when they'd first attacked her showed up in the distance and no matter how furiously she attempted to outmaneuver them, they slipped over, around, and through the barriers she put up in her system.

The mask came closer, cackling in that unnerving, unnatural voice it'd been programmed to use. And just when she thought she'd blocked it for good, a matching hand reached through her screen—smashing it—and dragged her inside her computer. They had her. She could never escape, and they were going to do a lot worse than steal some of her money.

Ruby screamed. And when the hand clamped around her wrists, pinning them above her head to keep her from mauling the masked man with her wildcat scratches, she thrashed and kicked instead.

Her knee connected with something solid and warm. "Oof. Ruby. Calm down. It's me, Ace."

"Ace?" She quit fighting as hard. He would never harm her. He wasn't the enemy.

"It's only a dream. You're safe." He blanketed her, stifling her attempts to lash out at the danger hunting her, real or imagined.

The weight of his body over hers—infusing her with his heat—woke all sorts of her parts, not only her mind. She blinked up at him in the light spilling into his bedroom from the nightlight in the bathroom. Half of her still shook off the enemies chasing her and the other half wondered what would happen if he lowered his head a fraction of an inch and their lips touched.

His bedroom door slammed against the wall. Both of them jumped. Ace whipped his head around in time to watch Liam come charging to their aid in a pair of black boxer briefs that hugged his hips and his package. *Damn.*

That helped take Ruby's mind off the monsters that had been pursuing her.

He scanned the room, gun held ready as he ensured no one had snuck into their living quarters in an attempt to maul her.

"It's clear, Liam," Ace reassured him. "She had a nightmare. That's all."

"Shit." Liam flicked the gun's safety on and set it carefully on the dresser. He ran his hands through his hair, which stuck up adorably as though he'd been tossing and turning since they'd gone to bed hours ago. He put his hands on his knees and drew in a few deep breaths as if he'd been as afraid as she had while in the grips of her dream.

"Sorry," she croaked. Shame and embarrassment eclipsed her terror, making her cheeks burn.

"No need to be." Ace drew her attention back to him and the way he'd caged in her body, protecting her from herself. He leaned on his good arm so he could brush errant hair from her face with his other hand. "Are you okay?"

"Isn't it obvious by now that I'm not?" She sank deeper into the mattress. In the dim light it seemed easier to say some of the things she'd been holding inside for a while.

Liam sat on the mattress beside them, causing it to dip some. He joined Ace in petting her, running his hands through her hair and down her arm. If they thought they were soothing her, they were dead wrong. She arched instinctively beneath Ace, her head tilting back and exposing her neck to him. When her torso lifted and pressed against his, the thin cotton of her panties and his shorts made it obvious that he wasn't unaffected either.

"Ace...careful," Liam warned.

And just like that, Ruby was robbed of Ace's heat. He rolled off her, cursing.

"Sorry, I didn't mean to get carried away." Ace used her poop emoji pillow to hide his hard-on, which would have made her laugh under other circumstances.

"Because you're already in a relationship with Liam?" she asked quietly as she retreated too, propping her shoulders against the headboard as she drew the covers up to cover her chest and her pebbled nipples.

She would have sworn she heard the pounding of the big guy's heart, though maybe it was only her own she picked up on.

"No. We're not..." Liam shook his head.

Ace winced as if he'd been kicked in the nuts and she

had a feeling he didn't need her pillow anymore. What the fuck? What were they hiding for? Even if they weren't interested in her, she'd thought they were friends. "Do you think I'm some kind of judgmental asshole?"

"Of course not." Liam tugged on his hair then scrubbed his hands over his face.

"Then be honest with me. It's not like Jordan cares if people on the team have relationships. Everyone's screwing everyone around here." She tried not to pout. "Except me."

Ace groaned and Liam stood as if the idea propelled him from bed with them.

"Go ahead, Liam." Ace seemed annoyed now too. Great, she'd pissed them both off. "Tell her what we are then."

"Nothing," Liam continued to lie, if only to himself.

"Um." Ruby bit her cheek, then decided to go for it. "My bedroom is directly on the other side of this wall."

"You're not going home, Ruby. Not yet and definitely not by yourself. If you want me to call Sola or Kennedy or someone else, I'll have them come get you and take you to their—"

"Calm down, Liam. I don't want to leave." Ruby spilled the truth before she could think better of it. "I can hear it when you guys go at it in here. Even with James overbuilding this place, there's no amount of insulation or soundproofing that's going to block out moans and thumps like that. You know that, don't you?"

"What?" Liam stumbled backward. He seemed as horrified by her disclosure as she'd been by the brutes chasing her in her dream.

"Whoops." One corner of Ace's mouth kicked up in a grin.

"So are you boyfriends? Or fuck buddies?" She put her hand over her mouth. "Sorry, you don't have to tell me. I've just...spent a lot of nights wondering."

Ace blew out a sigh that fluttered the dark hair dusting his forehead. "Liam's right. We're nothing. I'm convenient for him, that's all."

"Is that really what you think?" Liam asked, his head cocked.

"Am I wrong?" Ace fired back.

"I—" Liam shook his head. "I don't know anymore."

He edged toward the door, clearly in full retreat.

"Running away?" Ace sneered. "Doesn't seem like you."

"I need...a shower." Liam growled as he left the room.

"Funny, I'm pretty sure you're the cleanest person at Shields headquarters these days." Ace flopped to his back on the bed when Liam disappeared anyway. "Fuck my life."

"I'm sorry, Ace." Ruby wasn't sure what he'd welcome. Her company, her nosy meddling, or even a hug. So instead, she sat huddled at the top of his bed, afraid to step wrong again.

"You know what? I'd pretend I need to take a shit, but I'm not the fucking coward around here, now am I? I need a minute to myself." Ace rolled from bed and locked himself in his bathroom.

"Well, that went pretty good," Ruby whispered to the navy and gold dragon stuffie beside her, hoping it understood sarcasm.

She took a minute or two or ten to come down from the mixture of extreme emotions she'd flown through from fear, to desire, to embarrassment, to jealousy, and finally to sadness.

It was a lot to process.

She might have stayed lost in her thoughts a while longer except she realized she needed to pee. *Damn it.* Ruby got up and knocked on the bathroom door, but Ace either wasn't listening or didn't intend to answer. Great.

She thought about running over to her place, but although she thought the risk to be nearly nonexistent, she wouldn't break protocol like that. So instead, she jogged over to Liam's room, which mirrored Ace's in their apartment's layout.

The sound of running water didn't help her situation, so she tapped on the door and called his name urgently. "Liam? Hey, do you mind if I come in and pee quick? I'll be fast. Ace is in the other bathroom."

No response.

So she tried the door handle and it turned.

Steam billowed from the crack as the door inched open. The sink was to the right and beyond that, before the ginormous shower, was a separate toilet room. She'd sneak in, pee, and leave before he even knew she was there.

Ruby darted through the main area of the palatial bathroom and shut herself in the small space. After taking care of business, she prepared to do the same in reverse.

But when she opened the door, Liam was right there, in front of her. Okay, so he was really across the room, in the shower, but he was all she could look at. Especially as he stood—his back against the wall, warm water and soapsuds sliding down his gorgeous body—while he fisted his fully hard cock.

She would have slammed her eyes shut and made a run for it, no way was she brave enough to announce herself after what had just happened, except the glint of silver between his fingers caught her attention.

Was that...?

Ruby took a tiny step from within the toilet room into the main area of the bathroom. Her mouth dropped open and a hand cupped over it, muffling any sound she might have been able to make given her shock.

"I thought spying was our job," Ace murmured in her ear, refusing to let her go or turn away now that she'd been caught.

Ruby couldn't say what caused her to go limp in his grip. Maybe it was the intensity of the situation, or the desire that had been building within her every time she listened to the guys having sex, or the attraction she thought she detected between them over the past several months. Either way, with JRad's advice and her friends' encouragement fresh in her mind, she decided it was time to see if they were right.

What she'd been doing hadn't been getting her where she wanted to go. So it was time to try something different entirely.

"He's gorgeous, isn't he?" Ace whispered as they stared together in Liam's direction.

Ruby nodded. She wished she could tell Ace that he was every bit as handsome in his own way.

He used his grip to position her so that her back was plastered to his cut abs and chest. "You know what I realized, when I was thinking a few minutes ago..."

She angled her gaze to the side so she could meet his.

"You didn't seem to mind the idea of him and me fucking. No, you got off on it, didn't you?" Ace had never shown her this side of him before. Hell, maybe he'd never let it out at all until then.

There was no denying it. Ruby nodded as best she could, given his hold.

He smiled slowly then. "Well, maybe it's time for a little payback. Let's twist Liam up as bad as he does to us without even trying."

She nodded again.

Ruby didn't like the thought of being vindictive, but neither was she about to stop Ace when his free hand drifted over her breast, squeezing, before continuing to her mound. He cupped her over her panties, making her thrust against his hold.

She was no virgin, but she'd never had sex with a man like Ace and certainly not where anyone else could see if they simply opened their eyes. A dweeby computer nerd throwing her a quickie after a college lab hardly counted compared to the intensity of being in Ace's arms.

This...this kind of connection and all-consuming passion was what she'd dreamed of when she'd eavesdropped on them.

Ace nudged her panties to the side and ran his middle finger along her slit, making her whimper.

"Damn, you're soaked." He raked his teeth along her neck, then pressed the blunt tip of his finger to her entrance and worked it inside. Pumping it in and out, he fucked her in time to Liam's strokes along his shaft. She was surprised that as hard as he was, and as fast and rough as he was being, that he kept going so long. Weren't guys supposed to have hair triggers? Especially when solo?

"Why do you think he hasn't come yet, Ruby?" Ace asked. If he expected her brain to be functioning as he held her on the brink of orgasm, he'd be sorely disappointed.

Before she could answer, Liam did it for her.

"You think I can't hear you two out there?" Liam opened his eyes and stared directly at them. "This is a dangerous fucking game you're playing."

Ruby agreed. And it thrilled her.

"Are you sure this is what you want?" Liam asked as he shut the water off and stepped from the shower. He swiped water from his broad chest, abs, thick thighs, and the cock hanging heavy between his legs as he stalked toward them. He tossed the towel aside. "Answer me."

Ruby moaned and Ace added, "Shit, yes."

Liam fisted Ace's hair in his not-so-gentle grip. "Then make her come. Now. I want to watch her unravel in your arms, you lucky bastard."

Well, with an order like that after months of anticipation, Ace didn't have to work hard at all. The next time his fingers bottomed out in her, she shuddered around him. His other hand moved from her mouth to her neck so she cried out his name. Ruby would have fallen as her orgasm washed through her if Liam hadn't been there to brace her for Ace.

She hadn't even finished shuddering when Liam said, "Get on your knees, Ace. You're not going to be done after some shitty little finger fuck, are you?"

"No." Ace was already sliding to the floor between her knees.

Liam wrapped his arms around her and held her when her legs turned into wet noodles. He dangled her over Ace, who didn't need further instruction to understand what Liam wanted.

The wet heat of his mouth sucking on her still clenching pussy shocked her in the best of ways. She moaned and Liam swallowed it by crushing his mouth to hers. He paused only to mutter, "You two are going to be the death of me. Do you have any idea how long I've tried not to do this?"

"Why?" she asked, but quickly forgot why she cared when Ace began to eat her in earnest.

Her head lolled onto Liam's shoulder. When she opened her eyes and looked down, she nearly passed out from arousal. Both at the sight of Ace's face buried against her flesh and of Liam's hand still stroking, stroking that fat cock. From this close there was no denying what she'd glimpsed before. He was pierced. And not only once.

A row of barbells ran up the underside of his shaft. Each pass of his fingers over the hardware seemed to tug and rub and add to the pleasure he was giving himself. Holy shit, she hoped they didn't expect her to last long because another climax was already gathering within her, even larger and more powerful than the first.

"Let it take you," Liam commanded. "He'll make you feel so good."

She wanted to tell him that it was him too. That they both did. But speaking was beyond her then. Ace didn't help when he added a swirl of his tongue around her clit to whatever he was doing between her legs. She had a wide variety of vibrators, but none of them had ever given her a sensation like he did then.

"That's right." Liam growled near her ear. "Show him how much you like it when he goes down on that pretty pussy."

Ruby wouldn't have said she was into dirty talk until the words came from him.

Ace groaned, pulsating her sensitive areas, only adding to her pleasure. She screamed, wondering if she would have been able to hear the sound if she'd been in her own bed. Grateful that she wasn't, that she was finally here, in their arms, sandwiched between the two men she'd adored for a while even if she hadn't allowed herself to admit it...she came apart.

Ruby undulated in Liam's hold but he never wavered, holding her where Ace could feast.

She came on his face, riding his tongue and lips as she shattered so completely she wasn't sure she'd ever recover. Liam shifted her so her weight was predominately on one of his hips. He clutched her with one hand as his other flew over his cock.

"I have more for you, Ace," Liam rasped, his voice deeper than she'd ever heard it.

Ace gave her one last lingering kiss before turning toward Liam. He opened his mouth as if to suck the other man's cock but never got that far.

Liam roared, then emptied himself in white slashes across Ace's face, lips, and into his mouth. His fist flew over his cock, pumping every bit of seed from his balls, onto Ace.

And before the last drops of come had flown from his tip, Ace was joining them.

His cock—longer and thinner than Liam's and every bit as impressive—jerked before he shot his load all over his abs with a streak or two reaching up onto his chest.

Ruby shuddered in Liam's hold, trying to find her footing even as powerful aftershocks wrung her from the inside out as she watched their display.

"Son of a bitch!" Ace cursed as his release ebbed and he began to sag.

"You got her?" Liam asked as he handed Ruby to Ace. She could mostly stand on her own, but she leaned on his shoulder even as he clutched her as if he needed her support too.

Ace nodded. Liam went back to the shower and retrieved his warm, wet washcloth. He crouched so that he could clean Ace off, starting with his face, which glistened with their combined fluids, and then his body.

Ruby wondered if he was as sad as she was to see the proof of what they'd done wiped away from his skin. She tried desperately to catch her breath and keep the room from spinning, but it was no use. Ace was there to hold her when she sank into his arms. If it hurt him, he didn't complain one bit.

Liam swiped his thumb over Ace's lips, removing the last speck of their arousal, then stuck it in his own mouth, sucking it clean with a pop. "You should take Ruby back to bed. There are only a few more hours until dawn and her next shift."

"You're not coming with us?" Ace asked, his confidence slipping a hair even as he rose, refusing Liam's assistance.

"Not if anyone here is going to get some sleep." Liam shook his head, then strode toward his room, shutting them outside.

"Ace..." Ruby reached up to cup his cheek. She squirmed, but he held her tight to his chest.

"It's fine," he snapped, though it obviously wasn't. It couldn't be when Liam wouldn't admit what they shared. Instead of focusing on the pain, he seemed to use her nearness as a balm. He carried her back to his room.

This time when he laid her on his bed, it wasn't on the edge. It was in the center.

Ruby had zero complaints when he snuggled up next to her and wrapped her in his heat and hardness. "I have nothing to say for him. I don't get how he can walk away like that. I'm sorry I let him do it to you too."

"You're not responsible for his decisions, Ace." Ruby kissed him, thrilled to have the right and even happier when he kissed her back. "There's time to figure this out. And for tonight, I'm perfectly content to be here with you."

"I don't think anyone's ever said that to me before." Ace relaxed, maybe fully for the first time she could remember. "You're good for us, Ruby. We just have to make his stubborn ass admit it."

"A problem for tomorrow, Ace."

He squeezed her tight. "No matter what happens, I swear I won't ever treat you like he treats me. I care for you, Ruby. I wouldn't have fucked around with you even a little if I didn't. I don't know what that means for us or the rest of the tomorrows we have here at Shields, but that's the truth and I'm not afraid to say it."

Ruby might have cried if she hadn't already done enough of that in the past two days to last a lifetime. So instead she held him as tight as he was holding her. "You'll never have to wonder where you stand with me, Ace. I care about you too. Thanks for…"

"The orgasms? Anytime." He grinned.

"Seeing the real me." That was sappier than she cared to admit, but she wanted him to know—unequivocally—that she wasn't only using him for his cock, or his mouth, or his talented fingers. Especially if Liam had never given him similar reassurance.

"Same, Ruby. Same."

7

———

Ruby admitted there might be something to this *rest* thing. Especially if a couple of explosive orgasms followed by a night of snuggling with Ace—who was essentially the equivalent of a very sexy, very muscular, very toasty, life-sized stuffie that hugged back—counted. If he were a cartoon he'd be a golden retriever who also knew a thousand ways to murder his enemies but preferred to lick his friends instead. Literally.

He might be dangerous to criminals, but to her... Okay, so he was probably also hazardous to her heart. Now that she'd had a taste of what things could be like between them, it might kill her if she didn't experience more sexy times and a deepening emotional connection to go with them soon.

Still, she'd already made two important unlocks since she'd rejoined JRad in the command center. And was about to...*aha*! "I've got it, JRad. I know what they fucked up."

Even better, she thought the answer gave her a clue as to their identities.

"You do?" He swiveled to face her briefly before turning back to his screen. "Show me, please? My brain is melting trying to figure it out."

Ruby laughed. She actually fucking cracked up. In the middle of the madness and amidst the highest stakes of her career, she felt like she was on some ridiculous high. "Maybe I should make you wait as payback for siccing Liam on me last night."

"Are you going to try to tell me you didn't enjoy whatever happened after they dragged you out of this room?" JRad raised a brow at her, his full authority mode aimed in her direction.

"We both know that would be a lie, even if it wasn't exactly how I'd imagined it might go..."

"They need time. Especially Liam. He hasn't fully accepted his nature yet." JRad shook his head. "It's not easy to balance your need to be in control with life's uncertainties. He's running scared."

"Liam isn't afraid of anything." Ruby scoffed at the mere idea.

"He's terrified of Ace. Well, I should say he's freaked out by the thought of being unable to prevent something bad happening to the guy. I'm sure adding you to the mix isn't going to make his possessive instincts settle down either. I'd like to be wrong about this, but prepare yourself, because I think things are going to get worse before they get better." JRad was serious then. "But I'll say this, I believe they're decent guys even if they have no idea what the hell they're doing with each other—or you—yet. I'm always here if you need to talk. So is Lily if you prefer a woman's perspective."

Maybe on her next break she'd take him up on that and call his wife. Lily sure knew a hell of a lot more about men and what drove them than Ruby did. "Thanks, I think I might do that."

"How long have you been into them?" JRad asked, without a doubt it was true.

"A while." She shrugged.

"Oh so you're finally admitting it?" James asked as he joined them in the command center, looking like he'd had plenty of "rest" himself. Between his husband, wife, and the remainder of his crew...he probably had.

"Shut up." Ruby put her face in her hand.

"You've made more progress in a single day than me, Sola, Kennedy, and Laurel have in months of trying to knock some sense into these three." James hopped up on the table, his feet swinging as he teased her, and JRad grinned.

They probably would have relented and ended up giving her some high-fives before she dove into demonstrating her findings for JRad if James hadn't sat up straight right then. "Uh oh."

"I hate *uh oh*s." JRad grimaced.

Tavish went over to the window and groaned. "Double uh oh. Looks like someone's about to get their ass kicked."

JRad and Ruby ripped their headphones off and stood so they could see whatever it was that James, Tavish, and Legend were staring at. When she moved toward the window, she got a glimpse of Liam and Ace facing off in the parking lot. From the way Liam bristled, and Ace flung his hands in every direction while he shouted, Ace was confronting his partner. And she had no misconceptions about what. "Oh no. No, no, no."

"What the hell are they doing outside, distracted as fuck?" JRad growled. He turned to Ruby and shook his head. "I take it back, they might not be ready for you yet."

"This is probably my fault." James winced. "They were arguing in the lobby when I passed them and I was afraid Ruby might hear, so I told them to knock it off or take it outside. I didn't mean literally."

He pinched the bridge of his nose. "I thought they'd head to the gym to work out their aggression."

They might have let the two men hash out their issues, except just then Ace's fists balled. Ruby couldn't hear what he was yelling, but she'd never seen him angry like that before. Her instincts kicked in. He'd been there for her, to comfort her when she'd been attacked and also last night. No way was she going to let him stand on his own, especially if he was taking up for her along with himself.

Nor did she care to be the reason these two best friends developed some kind of unhealable rift. Not happening.

She bolted for the door, her hair bouncing against her back and the top of her ass as she sprinted toward the disaster unfolding in the rear parking lot.

"Ruby, wait!" JRad hollered, and James called after them as he too joined the parade of people intending to intercept the partners, who seemed on the verge of beating the shit out of each other.

When Ruby burst from the door, she immediately wished she still had her headphones on to avoid hearing the accusations Liam and Ace flung at each other.

"You let everyone else make themselves vulnerable but you're too good for that yourself. Fuck you. You're not going to take affection from Ruby without giving it back. It's not only about getting off to her. I'm not your goddamned clean-up crew."

Ruby lurched as if Ace had punched her in the gut. Was that how he'd felt last night? Like he'd had to tend to her after they'd had her fun. Was she some obligation he was too polite to ditch once he'd found relief?

"Are you talking about Ruby, or yourself?" Liam snapped, neither of the men even noticing that they had a growing crowd. "Don't use her as an excuse. I told you, more is not possible between us. It's fucking stupid and could get one of us killed."

"You're not going to have to worry about dying in the field if you keep taking advantage of Ruby. And, yeah... fine, me too. You giant fucking asshole." Ace did take a swing then, but given it was his bad arm, Liam absorbed the impact, grunting without fighting back.

Ruby flew between them, Ace's hand narrowly missing her cheek as he went for Liam again.

He froze, then turned a sickly shade of green when he realized that he'd nearly clocked her instead of his partner, whom he often scrapped with when practicing hand-to-hand maneuvers.

Legend and Tavish were only a few steps behind her. Legend grabbed Liam, who sagged, the fight going out of him as Tavish ushered Ace to the grassy edge of the lot where he looked like he might get sick. Left standing alone where they'd been, Ruby reeled.

It wasn't until she heard the screech of tires that she realized the fight between the two men she'd enjoyed so thoroughly the night before wasn't going to be anywhere close to the worst part of her day. A van sped down the alleyway behind the Shields' headquarters and skidded to a stop in front of her.

Everything went into slow motion, the way Ace had once described missions to her when he'd been waiting for Liam to return and his arm to heal. She looked into JRad's eyes long enough to see them bulge. He roared her name and pivoted, changing course from heading toward Legend to help with Liam and instead sprinting toward her.

It was no use. He was much too far away to stop the two men who spilled from inside the van. One snatched her up while the other aimed a gun directly at JRad.

Ruby thrashed. She kicked and screamed, terrified that she might watch her mentor's skull explode like a ripe watermelon in the next instant even while she mentally rehashed every self-defense exercise Sola had ever forced her to endure.

"Try anything and I'll kill him. Every last one of them," her captor snarled in her ear as he dragged her backward to the yawning door of the van.

It might have been a threat, but she wasn't going to risk it. Ruby went limp and the asshole hoisted her over his shoulder, tossing her into the backseat of the van before hopping in and slamming the door. Bullets pinged off the exterior as the driver gunned the engine. She lost her balance and crashed into the side of the vehicle.

Seeing stars, she rose to her knees in time to look out the rear window of the van.

JRad, Lucas, and Legend had guns aimed at the retreating vehicle. The instant they saw her peeking out, they pulled back their weapons and pointed them skyward. They wouldn't risk her becoming collateral damage.

Fuck!

"Well, hello there." Her masked captor's smarmy greeting made her want to rage. But she stayed perfectly silent. "You can thank us later, Ruby. We're about to make you famous. We're going to make you disappear just like Satoshi Nakamoto."

Ruby rolled her eyes at the reference to Bitcoin's founder, who had mysteriously vanished. No doubt who had grabbed her. Her heart raced as she watched Liam, Ace, Legend, and Tavish vault into James's absurd neon boogermobile as he tossed them the keys. They looked enormous wedging themselves into the car, which was oddly suited for a pursuit.

After all, the Hot Rods had worked on the thing no fewer than half a dozen times by now, each visit ending up in souping it up more while adding protections. So she only half-died when the asshole who'd grabbed her aimed his gun at the trailing vehicle and opened fire.

She cursed and threw her arms over her face to block the safety glass raining around her. The wind whipping through the void where it had been was deafening. And even still, she could hear the supercharged engine of James's car racing after them.

Please, please, please. Let them catch us.

"What in the Go-Go-Gadgetmobile is that fucking thing?" her attacker grumbled as he unloaded on the car, which didn't have any trouble deflecting the shots. At least the guys were safe.

Ruby hunkered down, making herself as small of a target as possible as she tried to remain calm and recall every bit of training Jordan had insisted she have even though she never worked in the field. She tried to get her bearings with quick peeks out the ruined window, preparing herself to dive through it at any hint of them slowing down for a red light.

Unfortunately, her kidnappers weren't that foolish.

They plowed through the center of Middletown, horns blaring as they narrowly avoided a collision in the main intersection. As they flew past Devra and Morgan's restaurant, a rumble joined the revving of James's car. When she popped her head up for another glance, two motorcycles too fancy to belong to anyone other than the Hot Rides had joined the chase. Quinn. And Gavyn, she thought.

But still the kidnappers were taking pot shots out of the window.

Oh God. Unlike Liam, Ace, Legend, and Tavish, the guys on the motorcycles had no protection.

If someone—one of them or an innocent bystander in town—got hurt because of her, she would never forgive herself.

She waved them off through the back window. One of the assailants got lucky and took out a bike tire, sending Gavyn skidding to the shoulder. Son of a bitch!

Quinn looked at her then his friend and gave way, going to aid Gavyn. Liam sped up, his bumper nearly touching that of the van.

There was a point where she could clearly see Ace. The horror and regret etched on his face made her ache for them both. It was surreal. All she wished in that moment was that she could tell him how much she appreciated him being there for her lately—including both when he'd blown her mind the night before and when he'd defended her emotions moments before she'd been abducted.

In case it was the last chance she had to give him any peace at all, she blew him a kiss before the van swerved, sending her careening to the ground again. The impact knocked the wind out of her. She only roused when the shooter said, "You're not going to make that, man."

"No choice." The driver ignored his colleague's advice.

"Those assholes aren't fucking around and that car probably has a rocket launcher for windshield wipers."

For all Ruby knew it did. She was sure that if she hadn't been their cargo, Liam would have taken more extreme measures to stop their progress by now.

Ruby shoved herself upward and whipped her head around to look out the windshield. Which was when she saw it. A train. Heading right for them. The arms on the crossing were already mostly lowered, but they weren't stopping. And neither was it.

All of that only for her to die in this tin can. Shit.

She caught one final glimpse of Liam and Ace and a flash of neon green before they slammed on their brakes. The van gunned it, speeding up as Liam slowed. Ruby thought she heard a bellow from the open passenger side window of James's car. "RUBY! Stay strong! We're coming!"

But she couldn't say for sure because the thunder of the train nearly clipping the van's rear quarter panel made her ears ring for minutes afterward. She wasn't sure if escaping being crushed was better or worse than the fate she was about to endure, but she thought of Ace's instructions.

If anyone could find her, it would be them. The Shields.

But damn, she really wished she'd finished telling JRad everything she'd discovered right before they'd been interrupted. It would have made the odds of them hunting her down a hell of a lot better.

Ruby collapsed as the train and the green car she'd never again make fun of disappeared from sight. She felt like a sailor watching land vanish on the horizon. With no way back, all she could do was drift, and hope that someone would rescue her.

At that instant, she had some major regrets. Not the least of which being that she hadn't fucked Ace at least the night before when she'd had the chance.

Because this time it wasn't a nightmare he could wake her from.

The bad guys had her, and they weren't going to let her go without a fight.

8

———

Ace thought he might be sick. For the first time, he had a glimmer of understanding for what Liam had gone through when he'd watched Ace take the bullet that had shattered his arm.

The world's longest and slowest motherfucking train had ensured that after it had passed, there was no hint of Ruby's assailants. Though they'd surveilled the area, the nondescript van had disappeared, so they'd turned around and returned to Shields headquarters, stopping on the way to make sure Quinn and Gavyn were okay.

The shop owner and head mechanic of Hot Rides had risked their fool lives to try to stop the van when they'd recognized James's one-of-a-kind vehicle in hot pursuit while they'd been leaving Quinn's wife Devra's restaurant. Without the bulletproof vehicle surrounding them in a protective bubble, they could easily have been shot or worse. Ace would never forget that they'd done it anyway, even though they'd failed.

All of them had.

Ruby was gone.

And it was entirely his fault.

He must have made some strangled sound low in his throat where the acid assaulted his esophagus. Liam gripped the steering wheel of James's car, which Ace would never make fun of again, in one hand and used the other to squeeze Ace's knee. "Hold on. We're almost there."

Legend shifted. It might have been comical, how he'd squished into the microscopic backseat with his roommate Tavish, if the situation hadn't been so dire. "This is only a regroup, not a retreat. We're going to bring her home."

Ace nodded because nothing else was permissible. He'd search for her the rest of his life if it came to that.

Liam took the turn into Shields practically on two wheels. The instant the car lurched to a stop, Ace bolted from it with Liam, Tavish, and Legend only steps behind him. They blew through the front door and into the command center. From the grim faces and dead silence— pretty much unheard of in their headquarters—everyone knew exactly how dire the situation was.

Ace couldn't even look James in the eye when the guy smothered him in a hug. Worse, none of their teammates —Jordan included—acknowledged their reappearance, focused instead on the monitors of Ruby's empty workstation, their own shoes, or the spot outside where everything had turned to shit.

Were they in as much shock as he was, or were they pissed off at him?

Either would be understandable.

Maybe all this time Liam had been right. Fucking around within the team was a terrible idea. Not only because it could be complicated and messy if things went wrong but also because their emotions were one hell of a distraction that they very clearly couldn't afford. Not when so many people's safety relied on their judgment.

Ace turned toward Liam and admitted to himself that he'd sacrificed any hope of being with the other man as surely as they'd lost Ruby. Because there was no way in hell they were going to get past Ruby's abduction considering how Liam had nearly imploded when Ace had gotten hurt on what he considered his watch.

In less than twelve hours Ace had gone from living out his wildest fantasies to being trapped in his worst nightmares.

"Liam…" he tried, although he already knew it was no use.

"Not now." His partner shut Ace down before they could get into another fight. "Don't you see? I always knew this is what would happen. If they hurt Ruby—or worse—it's on us. *Me.*"

"It is." Jordan snapped his stare to them. "But not because you've been dancing around her for months as if that makes you less unfocussed than actually having a relationship with her. What the fuck were you doing drawing her out into the open like that?"

"I wasn't thinking. Obviously." Ace pounded the table. "I was acting on emotion."

"Hey. That's not a bad thing." James defended Ace then, coming to stand beside him with a hand on his shoulder. "I feel responsible too. I literally told you two to take it outside, but…you know…I was being metaphorical. You could have gone and beat the shit out of each other in the gym or something."

"Oh." Ace felt like an idiot. And as if he didn't deserve the two people he, even still, craved most in the world.

"There are plenty of agents here who've learned to balance their connection with their responsibilities. It's not easy." Sola looked at Aarav, and Ace would bet she was thinking about the time she'd stepped in front of their boyfriend, Cash, when Aarav had been about to put a hole in his skull. Before they'd realized Cash wasn't the evil bastard they'd believed him to be. "But it's not impossible."

"For me, it looks like it is. I didn't *want* to be right. That's just how things are." Liam groaned and sank into the chair next to Ace, putting his head in his hands. "People I care for get fucked up when I'm preoccupied by how hot they are instead of what's going on around us. I'm sorry, man. I'm sorry. For everything."

Ace knew right then that Liam was ending things between them. They'd never recover from this.

When he reached out, because it was impossible to ignore Liam's suffering beneath the flogging he was inflicting on himself, Liam dodged Ace's hand. His comfort. His touch.

That stung, even worse than it usually did.

"Enough of this bullshit. What can we do to help Ruby?" Liam asked, his voice raising.

Ace wondered if the answer was less straightforward than his partner wanted it to be. Of course she needed them to go after her, but that alone wouldn't suffice. He met James's gaze and nodded. The guy knew a hell of a lot about relationships and making them work, even when they were convoluted. Ace would think about that more after they found Ruby and brought her home. Because if they couldn't do that, then none of the rest mattered.

Ace would never get over it. He'd become...Liam. Closed off and terrified of being destroyed when he turned out to ultimately be the one responsible for putting someone he cared for in harm's way.

Ah, shit.

It was impossible to be angry when he could relate.

Jordan looked as if he might press the issue, but instead he shook his head then turned back to observe their guest computer whiz, who was frantically scrolling through a text file that looked like it contained plain English notes rather than code.

"JRad—" A man of action, Liam couldn't wait another instant. Ace got that too. He felt utterly useless without someone to fight. Without any way to take even a baby step toward reclaiming Ruby from the bastards who'd snatched her from right beneath their negligent noses.

"I'm on it, guys. Swear. Sent the plate info from the security cameras to the Men in Blue for them to run it, though I'm assuming it's stolen." JRad didn't take his stare from his monitor for one nanosecond. "Now I'm working from this end. Right before you idiots started walloping each other and thoroughly sidetracked her, Ruby was about to tell me something she'd figured out. She fucking knew what was wrong with this shit and even how to fix it. She told me the code somehow led her back to the assholes doing this. I need to find what she saw and hope I'm half as smart as she is so I can interpret it like she did." He pulled her screen up next to his.

"You've got this." Jordan tipped back in his chair, seemingly unconcerned. Whether it was a show for Liam, Ace, and the rest of the Shields' sakes, or because he had absolute faith in JRad's abilities, Ace should have trusted his boss's opinion.

Though Ace didn't breathe for what felt like hours but

was probably only five minutes, it wasn't long before JRad hissed, "Yes! *Fuck* yes."

"You see it too?" Kennedy sat up straighter from where she'd been leaning against Marcus while Knox hovered protectively over them both. She was as worried sick as the rest of them, even if they were trying to focus on the job at hand instead of the oily terror winding through their guts now that one of their own was in the hands of their enemies. Marcus squeezed her hand.

"Hell no. Our girl is brilliant. I never would have spotted something this innocent looking. But she documented it for us." JRad beamed over his shoulder. "She doesn't need us. She's going to save herself with these notes she left behind."

"Explain," Jordan ordered.

More typing and a flourish of JRad's wrist before he used his index finger to poke the enter key with enough force for a dozen returns. When he did, a series of numbers appeared on the screen as if that would illuminate them.

"What is that?" Ace relied on every bit of training he had to stay calm when he wanted to run, he wanted to rage...do *anything* to reclaim Ruby. If he did, he didn't intend to let her out of his sight or his bed for a long damn time. That was...*if* she wanted anything to do with him anymore.

"It's sort of like a network address and it contains a unique identifier. Their sequences weren't mutating every block they attempted to corrupt because there's a location indicator embedded in here that didn't match the one of the computer that wrote the original block. She pinpointed where she could make a change so that the code would mimic the variable, and essentially debug their virus for them."

"I honestly don't give a shit about that stuff right now no matter how many billions of dollars are at stake." Liam had far less patience than Ace and he was running awfully short himself. "How can we use that to find her? Ruby is worth more than any pile of cash."

"It can be tied to an IP, and though they did some fancy footwork to cloak their true identities and origins, *that* I do know how to figure out." He grinned as his fingers assaulting the keyboard caused a clatter. His approach was brute strength as opposed to Ruby's grace. Now that Ace had someone to compare her to, he could tell how smooth and precise she was when she worked.

"So in non-geek speak, you're telling us you know where they're taking her?" Ace would have laid a wet kiss on the guy's scruffy cheek if he thought his legs would hold his weight right then.

"Generally." JRad pulled up a map. He grew still.

"What? What now?" Liam rasped.

"Maybe this wasn't as random an attack as we thought. They're not far from here. The odds of that are…"

"Implausible." Jordan shook his head. "They were stalking her. Teasing her with that code, weren't they?"

JRad nodded. "It was a trap. They knew who she was and where to find her all along. They aren't as good as she feared. They're manipulative bastards."

"To what end?" Jordan asked JRad.

"They need her to fix it." He flicked his mouse across the table before using his finger in the air and some technological wizardry to enlarge the map on the curved display so they could all see it clearly before he drew a neon yellow circle on the map, right over the campus of Middletown's college. "She's somewhere here."

"Let's go. I'll kick down every fucking door in the place until we have her. Before they move her or realize we're on to them." Liam practically vibrated with unspent energy as he shot to his feet.

"Sit down. The last thing we want to do is scare them off. We need to be more targeted. We're scalpels not grenades." Jordan shook his head and paused until Liam grudgingly did as their boss directed. "What else can you tell us, JRad?"

"I'm looking at the code they used. Ruby was in the middle of typing out a note on how to turn it against them like they did when they invaded the Shields system. And if I can pull that off...we might be able to see inside their—"

Before he'd finished his sentence, a live feed from a shitty quality security camera occupied one of Ruby's monitors. And there, far more chill than any of them, sat Ruby.

Her long vibrant red hair reached nearly to her pert ass and she slouched, one foot on her opposite knee, as if she was bored by being kidnapped.

"She's a good actress." Aarav sighed as they observed she was at least physically unharmed for the moment.

Fully occupied by staring at Ruby, his heart pounding in his chest, Ace didn't realize James had left his side to reclaim his own workstation. The other guy started executing image searches of campus, digging through social media profiles of alumni, and downloading brochures for prospective students then displaying results so they could see them in relation to the beige cube where Ruby was being held.

None of the rooms appeared exactly like the spot she was in. Painted cinderblock walls without a window in sight made Ace wonder if she was being held in a basement. Before he could speculate out loud, a door on the wall opposite from where she was sitting opened.

A man entered wearing a mask that matched the one his avatar had sported the night he'd attacked Ruby. It was only because Ace knew her intimately that he saw her freeze momentarily as if her image onscreen had glitched. She was scared, even if she didn't show it.

Stay strong, Ruby. He's a coward. You're not.

Two scrawny late-teens with bad complexions and that gangly, not-yet-bulked look to them trailed the masked man and slithered into seats at nearby computers as if familiar with the space. Whoever they were, they were certainly in over their heads.

"I have an offer for you." The masked guy didn't bother with pleasantries though he acted as if he was giving her a gift instead of what they all understood was an ultimatum.

Ruby didn't bother to respond.

"Help us finish the code these dumbasses can't fix and we'll cut you in." The guy, who wasn't particularly big or tall, crossed his arms as if that would help him seem more impressive. After hanging out at Shields, around massive men like Liam and Legend, Ruby didn't seem any more impressed than Ace was.

"You're saving this camera feed, right?" Jordan asked JRad.

"Yeah." He nodded.

"Any chance we can send it off for someone to analyze this asshole's voice or anything else about him. Maybe that watch, it seems kind of chunky." Jordan leaned in and squinted as if that was going to do the trick.

"Nah, it's utter garbage." JRad grimaced. "I mean, we can try but the odds are miniscule."

"If there's a chance, do it." Liam rocked as if his insides ached.

But Ruby, she was holding her own.

"Yeah, right. You won't even show me your face and you play dirty. Why should I trust you when you could steal my work then get rid of me?" Ruby tossed her mane of fiery hair over one shoulder.

"Firstly, because you don't have many options at the moment," the man snipped, his fingers digging into the arms of his suit jacket. "But also because we're talking about a lot of money. You have to know how valuable this is. Even a tiny cut is a shit ton of money."

"What are you going to wring people for?" Ruby acted as if she hadn't already heard it straight from Jordan. It was a good way to gauge how truthful the bastard was being with her.

"She's smart, our girl." JRad nodded as he kept furiously pounding his keyboard.

"Half a billion. And we'll give you a quarter of it if you help us."

"That cheap bastard." James rolled his eyes. "They could have at least made it something believable instead of a pittance."

Ruby lifted her chin but didn't give anything away as she stared at her captor with pure disdain. Ace was glad she'd never aimed that look at him. Though she likely would *when* they got her back.

"So what do you say?"

"Go fuck yourself." Ruby clearly included both the

masked man and his brutes guarding the door to her makeshift cell in her directive.

Sola groaned. The rest of the agents tensed. They knew where this was going.

"If you won't be reasonable, we'll use other methods to persuade you." The man in the mask gestured and one of the gunmen who'd captured Ruby lashed out, backhanding her before she even had a chance to brace herself against the blow. For one instant, the computer nerd nearby looked like he might object, but he quickly hung his head when it seemed like he could be next. The masked man redirected his attention to Ruby and snarled, "You should take the money, bitch. Speed up the process."

Liam clutched the boardroom table in his hands so hard Ace expected it to explode in a shower of splinters.

"Like you'd ever actually pay me a cent." She sniffed despite the trickle of blood staining her mouth like macabre lipstick. "I'm not helping you with shit."

This time the help clocked her with more than his open palm. Ruby tipped out of the chair, sprawling onto the floor. She landed on all fours and stuck there for a moment before she shook her head, sending her hair shimmering around her in a glossy curtain as she regained her wits.

Liam roared and stood so fast his chair flipped behind him. Ace knew it pained him far worse to watch her suffer than it would if he had taken that fist to the face. He was the sort of man who'd lay down his life for the people he cared about. He'd been meticulous lately about barricading the parts of himself that were even more vulnerable than his sexual side.

Ace had a sneaking suspicion Liam had erected his

defenses because he was feeling some kind of way about Ruby.

And maybe Ace himself. Though Ace had started to lose hope on that front.

"That's it. Enough, Jordan. I'm going. You can give me more specific directions on the way, but I refuse to sit on my hands while someone is laying theirs on her. Fuck this." Liam shifted his blistering gaze to Ace. "You with me?"

"Always." Ace hopped up and matched Liam's stride as they snatched the comms James tossed to them out of midair. He wouldn't have cared if Jordan ordered them to sit this time, nor would he have given a fuck if he'd been fired for going after the woman he was in hardcore lust with. But this time their boss didn't object.

"Bring her home." Jordan nodded to them. "Take Tavish and Legend since the four of you fit so well in James's car. What it lacks in discretion it makes up for in speed and tactical modifications I hadn't fully appreciated until today. We're going to need to talk to the Hot Rods guys after this is over. Sola, Aarav, Marcus, Knox, and Kennedy will follow in one of our unmarked vehicles as backup. Nolan, Ransom, and Levi will take an alternate route in case you all hit another roadblock."

Tavish groaned but didn't argue. It would probably be funny later that they'd gotten stuck in the spinach can. But for now, the entire team focused on one thing, rescuing Ruby before those fuckers could harm another one of the beautiful hairs on her head.

At the last second, Ace swerved and dashed to Ruby's station to grab her holographic unicorn stuffie. He had a feeling she was going to appreciate having it to cling to *when* they found her. He wouldn't blame her if she never trusted him to hold her and stave off her fear again.

If he'd had time, he'd have dashed upstairs and grabbed her poop emoji pillow instead. After all, the situation had turned into one hell of a shit show.

In the car, they tapped into both the headset audio stream and the video feed from Shields, which played on the dash display. As much as Ace wished he didn't have to witness Ruby's torture, he couldn't peel his eyes away from her.

"You're going to get on that computer now?" the man in the mask asked as he pointed at a mismatched system, cobbled together from equipment nowhere near as impressive, sleek or organized as Ruby's own workstation. Nor as colorful without her rainbow gradient mechanical gaming keyboard. She loved that damn thing,

When the other asshole who'd taken her from them pulled out his gun, Ace shuddered. Liam revved the engine and tore out of their parking lot, heading toward campus on the fastest possible route, avoiding downtown and congestion and definitely trains.

Ruby wasn't a fool. With a weapon aimed at her, she raised her hands. "Fine. Fucking whatever. You want me to work on this piece of shit? I will. But don't expect miracles."

The truth was, their resident genius already had the solution to the puzzle they'd laid out for her. Ace didn't believe for a second she was going to reveal it to the bastards holding her, though.

Still, she made a great show of tapping around on the keyboard while one of the dweebs breathed down her neck and Liam raced toward her, eliminating the miles between them one by one. They'd be there in less than fifteen minutes, ten if Liam kept smashing the speed limit like he was.

"We're coming, Ruby. I hope you know that we'd never let them have you without a fight." Ace wished she had her own headset so she could hear his reassurances. But if she did, he'd already have been begging for forgiveness and promising he wasn't ever going to take a risk with her again. Not on the job, and not in their love lives.

If Ace had to end whatever the hell messy situation he had with Liam in order to move forward with her, he would do it. She wasn't playing mind games. She'd been honest about her attraction and receptive to not only his passion, but also his affection.

"Quit fucking glaring at me," Liam rumbled. "That didn't do us any good earlier. We need to be partners. United. For Ruby."

"Only for her." Ace swung his gaze back to the video. She was a true hero. Standing her ground against the evil fucks who had her, refusing to cave. Not for money or to save herself.

He felt himself fall a little harder for her in that moment.

He hadn't even really had time to process everything he'd learned in the past few days. Ruby didn't need their paycheck. She took potshots at bad guys when she could have been lying on a beach in front of her dream home instead. And now she was in the thick of it. Still causing havoc in her quiet, determined, ultra-intelligent way.

Not only was she screwing around pretending to fix the virus code, she must have been using her time at that computer wisely. They'd been fools to hand Ruby her weapon of choice.

It didn't take too long before Ace figured out what

exactly she was doing since it obviously wasn't helping out the bad guys. She wasn't typing a love letter or her shopping list.

"Guys. Hurry." JRad's voice held cautious excitement. "She's doing it. I told you. Ruby's saving her fucking self."

"What do you mean?" Liam barked.

"She's sending me an encoded address. One." Pause. "One." Pause. "Three." Pause. "R...e...d....r...i...

"Redridge!" James shouted. "I'm looking at a picture of a lecture hall at 113 Redridge Avenue. It looks as boring and dead inside as that architectural shithole. On a Sunday during break it will be deserted."

Liam didn't hesitate—he floored the boogermobile, which had far more oomph than it should. Their acceleration plastered Ace to the custom leather bucket seat. What the hell had the Hot Rods done to the thing?

They rocketed toward the coordinates that popped onto the onboard display. A 3D model of the building's blueprint appeared after it, temporarily obscuring Ruby from Ace's sight. He studied it, memorizing every detail he could. He might not have been Ruby's level of smart, but he had warrior skills.

"Another present from Ruby?" Jordan asked as the same diagram was likely broadcast on the command center screen and in the other two vehicles in pursuit, which couldn't quite keep up with James's supercar.

"Yeah." JRad confirmed before snorting as a circle appeared in the basement followed by a few slightly shaky lines.

Ruby drew a pink stick figure in the basement, as Ace had suspected, on the south side of the building with a cartoon speech bubble that contained the word *HELP!*

"Tell her we're coming," Ace begged JRad.

"Too risky to send a response the people over her shoulder could spot." He grunted. "Don't worry. She knows. *Everyone* knows the two of you would be hot on her tail no matter where in the world these bastards had taken her. Now don't fuck it up."

Shame sat heavy in Ace's gut. He deserved that. And he wouldn't make the same mistake again. This time, he was going to focus on protecting her, even if that meant from himself.

9

Ace flexed his fingers around the grip of his gun several times as he half-crouched, half-ran around the rear of the building to the service entrance he and Liam were about to use to infiltrate it. It had been months since he'd been in the field, but despite the worries he'd smothered while falling asleep most nights since his injury, it felt familiar.

The sound of his heart steady but strong, amplified by the comms in his ear. Liam in his peripheral vision as Ace scanned the area for signs they'd been made. The hope that if all went well, it wouldn't be long before they took one more piece of shit out of the world so they could never harm another person again.

His damn palms didn't lie, though—they were sweating around his weapon. What if he wasn't ready? What if his new weakness put Ruby at risk?

Maybe they should have waited for one of the other cars to arrive. Or maybe he should call Tavish to take his place on the lead team with Liam while Ace watched their sixes with Legend.

If he'd had another few seconds to debate and doubt, Ace might have done it.

But when he glanced at his partner, Liam jerked his chin toward the door. This was it. They were going in.

Together. Like they always had before.

Except Ace was scarred. Forever changed. And he couldn't afford to let his doubt claim a toehold on his focus or Ruby would pay for it.

Ace entered the six-digit code JRad had given them and the security panel flashed green. While it might have been more satisfying to bust the thing down, having stealth on their side for as long as possible was worth keeping Liam's aggravation pent-up. His partner practically vibrated with fury and the need to lash out.

Soon, he was going to have his chance.

Ace popped open the door and peeked inside. The boring paint color and cinderblock wall matched the one he'd been staring at on the video feed. No one there. A short hallway led to a corner. Around it, three doors down, was the room Ruby had indicated she was in. Damn, she was incredible. She'd literally given them a map. All they had to do was use it.

He wasn't about to let her down. Again.

He signaled to Liam with his free hand then ducked inside. They crept along the hall, listening for any signs of movement and heard none. So he kept going. Liam reached the corner first and checked around it, before beginning their final approach. One door, two...

She was there. Right there on the other side of the wall. Ace swore he could feel her energy—sparkly and special.

"Tavish. Legend. Stay alert. They're about to go in." James's steady voice alerted the rest of the team outside the command center to Ace and Liam's status as he watched the stream from their bodycams. "Guys, remember, we need the masked man alive if at all possible. The rest of the team will be there in five minutes, tops."

A lot could happen in that amount of time and no one was suggesting they wait.

Ace looked to Liam, who nodded. This was it.

Liam gestured toward the doorknob, so Ace took a deep breath. Then in one motion he grabbed it, turned, and flung the door wide. His own heart leapt as his partner, best friend, and sometimes lover rushed into the eye of the storm of danger, because that's the kind of man he was.

Time froze.

Was Ace afraid? More than he'd ever been before. Taking that bullet had impressed upon him the very real risks involved. Ones he maybe hadn't considered seriously enough when he'd been younger and the illusion of invincibility hadn't yet worn off. Now he knew precisely how small their margins for error were.

But he wasn't about to let Liam face those odds alone.

When Ace charged after him, entering the room, the two dweebs were still hovering over Ruby, though their puzzled expressions made it clear that even watching her every keystroke didn't clue them in to whatever she was doing. Beside them, one of the gunmen was leaning against the wall. And the other bracketed them, standing between the masked man and everyone else.

That left the masked man immediately in front of them, completely exposed. Ace's primal urge to take him out was something he'd never experienced before.

"Don't do it," Jordan warned in Ace's ear. "We need him."

The masked man knew it too. He barked at his gunmen, "Get rid of the evidence. But not her."

Liam elbowed the guy in his shrouded face, trying to stop the inevitable. As the man grunted and doubled over, Liam shoved him aside, flinging him so that he crashed into a row of desks. But he didn't make it through the asshole fast enough and the mercenary beyond him took out first one then the other dweeb with two rapid shots. Of course that also left his back turned to Ace and Liam, who returned the favor.

Ace ignored it all. His eyes locked on Ruby's for an instant before flicking to the second hired gun who held her captive. The brute had his arm around her neck by then, locking her tight to him. Those bastards needed her even more than the Shields needed the masked man. She was safe for the moment. But her captor...not so much.

Ace lifted his bad arm and braced the butt of his gun with the opposite hand.

He wasn't very far away and had nailed shots like this repeatedly during his training sessions since getting his cast off, and still, he wobbled.

While he and Liam were focused on Ruby—their primary objective—the masked man staggered to his feet and circled around behind them. He lunged for the equipment stacked in the corner and ripped an external drive from it. A cable still dangled from one end when he pivoted and sprinted for the door.

Ace whipped his gun from the guy clutching Ruby toward the masked man, then back. On former missions he'd have dropped one then the other, fast enough that neither would have been able to cause a problem. Worse, to compensate for Ace's uncertainty, Liam had to cover him. The masked man reached the doorway.

Ace's hand wavered as he aimed for the man clutching Ruby again. He debated switching his grip to his left hand, but there simply wasn't time. And he hadn't practiced enough yet. Not when Ruby's face was inches from his target. "Shit!"

"Should I take the shot?" Liam barked.

It had only been a flicker of hesitation, but in their line of work. That was too much.

Instead of dividing and conquering, neutralizing both targets, Ace watched as Liam did what he'd gotten too in his head to accomplish. Liam fired, exploding the bastard threatening Ruby's skull. He was dead before he hit the floor.

Ruby tumbled to her knees only slightly slower. Ace wanted to rush to her side, but there was unfinished business. Both he and Liam switched their focus to the masked man, but he bolted into the corridor.

By the time they cleared the opening, he'd scrambled around the bend in the hallway so both Ace's and Liam's low shots—intended to take him down, not out—pinged off the corner of the cinder block wall. Neither hit their mark. Over the comms, Liam shouted to Tavish and Legend, letting them know the guy was heading for the exit even as he pursued the asshole.

Ace looked between Liam's retreating form and Ruby before Jordan's voice echoed in his ear. "Stay with Ruby. Cover her until this is over."

It was the easiest order Ace had ever followed in his life as he stumbled over the four corpses to where she huddled in an expanding pool of someone else's blood then planted himself between her and the doorway. He made himself much bigger than he felt as he became her human shield.

"Son of a bitch!" Ace heard Tavish shout over the comms. "There's some kind of tour happening out here. A group is approaching..."

"Fuck!" A thump accompanied Jordan's curse, making Ace wonder what he'd banged his fist into. "Pull back. No civilian casualties. Do not open fire."

"You want us to let him go?" Legend didn't seem to like that idea any more than Ace did by his incredulous tone of voice.

Ruby croaked, "I booby trapped the fuck out of that drive. We'll be able to pinpoint their location next time he plugs it in. And I made it so they can't copy anything off of there without scrambling the data either."

Jordan must have heard. He called the team off. "Fall back. We have what we need. Get Ruby and get the fuck out."

Ace had no trouble obeying that command. As Liam reappeared in the doorway, his shoulders filling the entire thing, Ace shoved his gun into its holster then spun and crouched beside Ruby.

Rather than shrinking from him or smacking his hands away like he feared, she launched herself into his open arms.

"I've got you," he promised as he stroked her hair and crushed her to his heaving chest. "You did so good. You're safe. We're getting the fuck out of here."

Over the comms, he heard Legend and Tavish setting up a diversion that would keep the tour from stumbling across their wreckage before the two teams arriving just then could dispose of it properly.

Ruby blinked at the bodies splayed around them, tears

welling in her eyes when her gaze shifted to the two stupid college kids who'd obviously gotten mixed up in something far more sinister than they'd realized, then buried her face in the crook of Ace's neck. "Take me home. I don't know how the rest of you do this. I'm made for my nice cushy workstation."

"I've got your unicorn in the car," Ace murmured to her. "We'll be there soon and you'll never be in danger again. Not like that. I swear. I'm so sorry, Ruby."

She didn't respond, though her breathing hitched. They hadn't solved the problem for good, but they'd made progress. And they had Ruby back. That was all that mattered.

Liam led the way, gun drawn, as they marched back to James's car. Ace handed Ruby to Liam long enough to climb into the backseat and then held his arms out. Liam deposited her into his lap where she settled, clinging to him as if he intended to ever let her go again. When Liam put her unicorn on Ace's chest, she squished it between them and sighed.

Tavish and Legend jogged to the car. Despite his black combat boots and matching kilt, Tavish managed to contort himself into the backseat beside them. Kennedy hailed them over the comms. "Does she need a doctor?"

Tavish studied Ruby curled up in Ace's arms and said, "Don't think it's medical attention she needs at the moment."

Ace tucked his chin against his chest so he could peer down at her and the faint bruise already appearing on her porcelain cheek. He winced.

"Okay, but I want to check her over as soon as we get home." Kennedy was a damn good medic. She'd ensure neither Ruby's body nor psyche had suffered too much damage.

Liam cursed under his breath. Ace understood. They'd gotten incredibly lucky. Things could have ended up so much worse. He tucked into the driver's seat and launched out of the lot.

The ride back was quiet, each of them lost in their own thoughts. Ruby never once stopped clinging to her unicorn or Ace. And when she started to shiver, he rubbed her back and arms in what he hoped were soothing circles.

This time they didn't stop in the lot. They pulled into one of the armored garage bays they usually only used when transporting bodies or soon-to-be bodies or other things they didn't want anyone to see hanging around headquarters. No one was taking chances.

Ace wasn't sure if he imagined it or maybe if it was an accident, but he swore Ruby brushed her lips over his neck before refusing help as she climbed from his lap and emerged from James's car. Sola and Kennedy were there to surround her and whisk her away to the medical area.

Even letting her out of his sight long enough for an examination felt like a horrible idea, but Ace didn't have much choice or any right to barge in and observe something that was technically none of his business.

Jordan, James, and the rest of the team headed for the command center for a debriefing and to plan their next steps. But Ace couldn't bring himself to follow. Was he an asset to the team, or a hindrance?

Lucas stepped out from the shadows in the garage, where he'd been leaning against the wall out of the way, next to JRad. His slightly uneven gait brought him closer.

Liam looked between Ace and Lucas without saying a single fucking word. How pissed was he?

"You have to trust yourself before anyone else will." Lucas squeezed Ace's shoulder, causing a groan to fall from his lips. It was true.

How could Liam have faith in him if he wasn't sure of himself? But how could Ace be confident when it was clear his partner didn't believe him capable of taking care of himself? They were caught in a vicious cycle.

JRad, on the other hand, concentrated on Liam. "You blew that. You know it, right?"

Liam cursed and kicked the tire of James's car. Of course that did nothing but punish his toe since the thing was clearly not standard road gear. "Yeah."

"Ace had that shot. He could have taken it in his sleep." Lucas seemed to support JRad's assessment. "I've only been to the range with him once and I know that, so you must too."

Liam nodded, swallowing hard.

"What you should have said was, 'Do it. You've got this.'" JRad shook his head as he scolded Liam. "If you don't step up and assume control, Ruby and Ace are only going to keep getting let down or worse. Take responsibility for them. Yes, it's fucking terrifying, but if you value their opinions, then recognize they are putting their loyalty—and whatever else—in you for a reason. Deserve what they're willing to give. Don't keep throwing away that gift or you're all going to get messed up even worse than you have been already. I don't think you have many chances left."

Liam nodded, but his brow was scrunched as if the advice was still attempting to penetrate his thick skull. They ambled into the headquarters and recapped the mission, agreeing that JRad would set up a monitoring system for whatever the fuck signal Ruby had embedded on the drive and apparently sent him information about while working at gunpoint.

She was incredible and Ace was sure then that his infatuation had evolved into something with greater significance than admiring her cute butt or chatting with her during group dinners. There was more to Ruby than he'd even realized before.

And he wanted her.

Whether or not Liam acted on JRad's advice, Ace intended to make the most of his last shot.

When Ruby returned, shoulders back, head high and a colorful cartoon bandage on her cheek, she seemed like she might have received some advice of her own. "Jordan, can I have Liam and Ace? I need to work out some stuff with them."

Their boss attempted to stifle his grin but it peeked out in a lopsided smile nonetheless. "Sure, Ruby. I'm glad you're okay."

She nodded. "I will be. Today was a good reminder that our time is up sooner or later and I don't plan to fuck around wasting any of it anymore."

JRad beamed at her. "I always said you were my best student."

Without meeting their gazes, Ruby spun around and headed out the door in the direction of the elevators. "Let's go, boys. We need to talk."

10

"I assume you don't want anyone else assigned to your protection?" Jordan called after Ruby.

She looked over her shoulder.

Rather than the defiance or hell-no attitude she expected Ace and Liam to exude as they tailed her out into the hallway, the wounded despair on Ace's face and the stony mask on Liam's told her they still had plenty to fix between them, even aside from the additional damage caused by that morning's events.

"Nah, boss. I'm good."

Ace lifted his stare and it locked on hers. He seemed incredulous, or maybe like he was doubting her sanity. Well, he shouldn't have. Being abducted and in very real danger of not surviving had shown her clearly what was important.

And she was looking at it.

There had been so many times in her life when she'd felt like too much. When she'd tried to make herself less dorky, less garish, less childish, or less brilliant to avoid intimidating someone or risk putting them off...especially guys. She was never going to make herself small so they could feel big again. Fuck that.

Ace would be able to handle that, she was sure of it. But could Liam?

They were about to find out.

"When Devon gets that tone of voice…" James clapped and gave an exaggerated shiver. "This is either going to be one of the best or worst nights of your lives. Have fun!"

Ruby might have bitten her lip if the damn thing didn't still sting. She ignored everything except the fire inside her that had been lit the night before. It blazed within her even stronger after nearly losing her chance to do anything about it. She marched toward the elevators, then stabbed the up button.

Behind her, she caught Sola's grumble as the guys filed out of the room. "Don't fuck this up."

Her friends were the best, honestly. They understood that no matter the bravado Ruby's near-death experience had instilled in her, underneath she was still the insecure nerd who'd never been asked to the prom or had a real boyfriend. A quick fuck in the computer lab after a study session to ditch her v-card hardly counted for much.

Ace's fingers inside her the night before, and his tongue on her most sensitive places—damn, his tongue— had brought her a hell of a lot more pleasure than going all the way with an underclassman for the sake of a scrap of experience.

Somehow none of that mattered, because like Kennedy had reminded her earlier, instinct counted for a lot. Hell, Ruby—along with pretty much everyone they worked with—had watched Kennedy lose her virginity on a mission. Of course they hadn't known it at the time and it was to Knox, the man she'd always loved and one of the two she still did.

It had worked out for Kennedy, and Sola, and Laurel, and all the other Powertools peeps surrounding Ruby every day. It could work for her too. It *had* to.

Ruby strode into the elevator, prepared to hold the doors for Ace and Liam. She shouldn't have bothered—they were right on her heels.

The instant the reflective metal slid closed, Ruby flung her arms around Ace's neck and thanked him properly for saving her ass. She practically climbed him right there in the elevator while Liam watched. Ace's hands cupped her ass as she wrapped her legs around his waist, clasped his skull between her still trembling fingers, and crushed her lips to his.

He kissed her back with equal parts fervor and apology.

Liam cursed under his breath but stayed put when he could have bracketed her between them. She'd barely gotten a taste of Ace when the door dinged on their floor and he stepped out, walking her to their apartment. Despite Liam's hands-off approach, he followed, letting them inside and locking up behind them.

No one could enter Shields' headquarters without their knowledge. Liam didn't seem to care. He cleared the living room, kitchen, then Ace's room and finally made his way to his own, Ace following him, before setting his gun on his nightstand.

Ruby wriggled from Ace's grip and he lowered her reluctantly to the ground. He shouldn't have worried; she wasn't going far. She closed the gap between her and Liam as Ace kept pace with her. The entire time, she met his golden stare unflinchingly.

"I thought you wanted to talk." Liam's eyes narrowed.

"By 'talk', I meant fuck." Ruby didn't hedge. If he pushed her away this time, she'd know he simply didn't share this desire she had for him and his partner.

Ace chuckled. He patted her ass as if to encourage her to keep going. She stalked Liam, taking two steps forward for every one he retreated. The idea that he might be afraid of her, or rather what she was offering, was nearly comical.

"You're high on adrenaline." Liam held her at arm's length. "You should wait until you come down from its effects before doing something you might regret. You aren't making rational decisions."

"Is that what you tell yourself? Or do you screw Ace senseless when you return from a mission and you realize you're both still alive when things could have easily gone sideways?" Ruby propped one hand on her hip. "That's a rhetorical question. The things I hear through the wall tell me everything I need to know. Why do you think that is, Liam? It's not because of some dumb chemical reaction. It's because you care about him. And it's about time you admitted it. To yourself, if not to him."

"Of course I care," Liam sputtered, his face growing ruddy. "We're partners. Roommates. Best fucking friends."

"You're lovers." Ruby refused to shade the truth, though he surely didn't need the reminder.

Neither did Ace's fully erect cock, which strained at the zipper of his jeans and brushed against her lower back as he edged up behind her. Sandwiched between two of the more powerful men she'd ever met, she might have been afraid, especially after what she'd so recently gone through.

Instead, she felt sheltered.

"Don't worry, Ace. I'm not going to leave you hanging like he does—physically or emotionally." Ruby reached behind her and cupped the prominent bulge there, making him groan. "I know I'm dorky as hell and you two are studs, but this doesn't lie. You want me and I'm not going to get in my head about it anymore."

She squeezed him, wringing a moan from him. And causing herself to wonder what the hell had gotten into her. Liam was partially right—her internal systems were still going bonkers after her near-death experience—but it was more than that. It was about finally being honest and unleashing the part of her that wished she'd been brave enough to do exactly this for the past several months.

"I'm into this. You're definitely into it. And so is Liam, even if he's still trying to pretend otherwise." Ruby sneered at him, refusing to pull her punches anymore.

"I'm not—"

"You are." Ace backed her up, inspiring her to rub his cock through his pants as a reward. "Sometimes you'll give in long enough to get us off, but that's it. And that's not going to cut it anymore. I want something more than orgasms, even damn good ones."

Ruby looked over her shoulder and smiled up at him, promising she was going to give him everything he desired. "I've got you, Ace."

He rested his cheek on the top of her head for a moment, hugging her from behind. But when she expected Liam to say something...anything...he only stared hungrily at them instead.

"For a while there, I thought Ace was the one who was broken. He's not. It's you, Liam." Ruby snuggled against Ace's side, loving when his arm—scars and all—looped around her shoulders and tucked her tight to him as if she belonged there. Because she was starting to believe she might.

"You know I don't have a lot of patience to begin with, and I'm running short. So are you in or out?" Ace asked his lover, or was it about to be his ex?

No, Ruby wasn't about to let Liam ruin the best thing in both of their lives.

"You're fucking in, you hypocrite." She scowled at him. "You keep saying you don't want to hurt us, but what the hell do you think you're doing? If not to me, then to Ace?"

Ace jerked and stared at her with wide eyes as if he never expected it would be *her* protecting *him*, but there she was, standing up to Liam even though he was easily twice her size.

Liam's jaw hung open. No sound came out so she kept pushing.

"Of all the places in the world for us to be, one of the safest is in your bed." Ruby took a step toward him, her hand snagging Ace's and dragging him with her as she stalked Liam. "There, only you have the power to wound us. So don't. Just don't."

His eyes flashed. "You sound like JRad."

"Not surprising." She shrugged. "I learned a lot from him. About computers, and also relationships. Spending time around him and Lily is...enlightening."

"Kind of like living here." Liam stared up at the ceiling and sighed. "We're surrounded by relationship experts. It isn't that easy for me. It freaks me out. Thinking of losing you."

"If you never claim us, then you're already going without," Ruby said as gently as she could when the urge to shake him bubbled within her.

Ace cleared his throat. "Stop holding back, Liam. Unless you think we can't take it."

Liam's pupils dilated and the noise that rumbled from his chest was as close to a growl as she'd ever heard from a man. Ace was antagonizing him and it was going to work.

Ruby curled the fingers of her free hand in the waistband of Liam's jeans. She intended to drag him with them if necessary, the hunger in his stare and his matching bulge to Ace's making it plain that he wanted to get naked as much as they did. Maybe more.

Instead, he clasped her hand in his much larger one. "You're sure this is what you want? I'm not cute and cuddly like Ace."

Ruby feigned shock. "No kidding. You've got much more in common with a grumpy grizzly than a teddy bear. Bring it on."

11

―――

Liam flashed a toothy smile that didn't change her opinion of his nature. Nor did it deter her. Ace wouldn't let Liam push her further than she would enjoy. She leaned backward against his chest, confident he would be there to support her.

Regardless of the uncertainty she'd seen flash across his face during her rescue, she didn't doubt him for a moment. Maybe after she was done with him, he could regain some of his cockiness. She'd wanted to hate that about him, but had secretly adored it from the moment he'd joined the Shields.

She smiled and tipped her face up. Ace didn't disappoint her or leave her hanging. Not when Liam had done the same to him far too often. He cupped her chin and brushed his thumb feather-light over the split in her lip. "Tell me if this doesn't feel good."

Ace licked her lower lip, then slid upward to fuse their mouths more completely. He was sweet and tender, and if it stung some, it only added an edge to his kisses. Ruby nearly got lost making out with him until Liam stepped closer, heat radiating from the wall of muscle he made in front of her.

"Damn, you're sexy together." He put a hand on the back of each of their heads and angled them so they could sip more deeply from each other. "Better than every dirty dream I've had of you."

Ruby's knees wobbled, but Liam was there, his hands easily spanning her waist, as he held her in place for Ace to feast on. Knowing he'd thought of her, and Ace, in the same lewd and wonderful way she'd fantasized of them, often waking on the cusp of orgasm that a few swipes of her fingers easily fixed, made it harder to draw in a full breath.

"Devour her, Ace. Let me watch the two of you. Tempt me to do things I know I shouldn't, even more than you already do." His admission was tortured. If Ruby had a single bit of processing power left when Ace blew her mind with strokes of his lips and tongue over hers, she would have confronted Liam about his misconception. There was no reason to withhold this pleasure from themselves.

It would have to wait. Because Ace's mouth on her wrecked her logic. All she could do was feel. And when Liam steered them to the side of his massive bed, she didn't resist. Not either one of them. She let them caress every inch of her from her shoulders to her neck to her waist and everywhere in between.

"Strip her," Liam commanded.

Ace opened his eyes long enough to verify she was on board. When she didn't object, he did as he was told, wasting no time in fisting the hem of her black T-shirt with the title of her favorite wuxia novel in red characters across the chest. He grabbed it and walked it up her abdomen. She wasn't cut like Sola or even softly rounded with womanly curves like Laurel.

Ruby was...average at best.

The guys didn't seem to mind.

"Show her to me." Liam backed up just enough that he could get a full view of her.

Ace nudged her until she lifted her arms. He stripped the soft, well-worn fabric from her, letting it fall, forgotten, somewhere behind them. Her basic beige bra was utilitarian but the intensity of Liam's stare made her feel as though she was wearing crystal-studded lingerie from a French boutique instead of whatever Middletown's general store kept in stock.

That's what she found so addictive about them. They acted like she was everything she'd always imagined being when she'd gotten lost in one of her epic fantasy novels. Someone sensual and feminine and powerful and innately desirable simply for being herself.

"More," Liam rasped, "Show me more."

This time Ace knelt. She steadied herself with her hands on his shoulders, impressed as always by how solid he felt beneath her fingers. Despite his recent injury, Ace was in better shape than pretty much anyone she'd met in real life before coming to Shields. He was capable even if he'd forgotten that about himself.

He stripped off her sneakers, socks, and jeans, leaving her standing before them in her underwear. Ace nuzzled the spot right above her mound, breathing deeply of her scent even as he cupped her ass and tugged her tight to his face. But when he reached for her panties, she balked.

"What's that about?" Liam asked when she shifted away from Ace.

Ace blinked as if he hadn't picked up on her

hesitation. He paused and looked to Liam for guidance. Their bond was natural and complementary. Ruby wasn't surprised they were such excellent partners both in and out of bed.

"It's nerve wracking being naked in front of someone who looks like you guys. Never mind two of you." Ruby swallowed hard.

"You're perfect, Ruby." Ace kissed every bit of her he could reach from her stomach to the tops of her thighs. "You're adorable and sexy at the same time."

"Give her what she needs to be comfortable." Liam shifted his focus to Ace. "Get naked. Now."

Ace didn't have to be told twice. He got to his feet, reached behind his head, and grabbed the back of his shirt, whipping it off in a single fluid motion that did funny things to Ruby's insides. And that was before she took stock of the black and gray ink highlighting the ridges and valleys of his rippling muscles.

He toed off his boots and stripped his jeans down his legs, revealing a patch of dark hair that led to his stiff cock.

"I thought you were a spy, not a commando."

Ace snorted. "See, you're funny too."

They might have joked around longer, but Liam wasn't about to let them get sidetracked. He stared at her, the intensity of his gaze making her draw in a deep breath. "Better?"

"Halfway." She couldn't believe she'd basically asked him to strip for her, but she figured it was the least of what she'd requested when she'd decided to be the aggressor and demand they act on the attraction that had been zinging between them for so long.

The corners of his mouth kicked up. "I like it when you're greedy."

Liam was more deliberate but not any shyer than Ace. He took off his black T-shirt and folded it, allowing her and Ace both to ogle him as his smooth golden skin was revealed. Unlike Ace, he didn't have a single tattoo, but it didn't leave him looking plain. No, he reminded her of a statue of the perfect male form she might have studied in a museum.

"Never gets old," Ace murmured to her as he hauled her close to him, his hard-on rubbing against her side.

But it was when Liam removed his jeans, adding them to the neat pile on his dresser, that she remembered the piercing she'd glimpsed the night before. A flash of silver piqued her curiosity. With his cock hanging heavy between his legs it wasn't very noticeable, but she intended to ask him a million questions about it later, when they weren't busy.

Liam strode to where she stood in Ace's loose embrace and smiled down at her. "Ready to ditch the rest?"

Ruby nodded, if only because she was going to burst into flames if they didn't touch her soon and she needed to be naked for them to do it right.

"Did I tell you to stop kissing her?" Liam cut his gaze to Ace, who groaned then resumed blowing her mind, this time sucking on her tongue to distract her while Liam unhooked her bra and peeled it from her. The air was cool on her skin for a moment before Ace plastered himself to her front. Liam, however, bent so he could rip her panties from her with a single jerk at each side seam.

Oh. Good thing she didn't invest in pretty ones.

Ace rocked against her, his cock painting a wet trail in the arc he traced on her belly.

"I can't believe we almost waited too long to do this,"

Ruby muttered when he let her catch her breath and instead feasted on her neck.

"Don't think about that," Liam instructed as he ran his fingers through her hair from her scalp to the top swell of her ass. "It doesn't do any good. We're here now. Enjoy it while you can."

She wanted to tell him the same but didn't have any desire to start a fight or do anything to keep the men from going further in their explorations together. "I intend to."

Ruby grabbed hold of the spark in the pit of her stomach, the one that had flared to life when she'd stared down the barrels of those assholes' guns earlier. She craved this. She wanted to make love to her neighbors and finally understand what it felt like to be caught up in the passionate exchange they'd so often had without her.

Ruby couldn't stand another moment of Ace's unintentional teasing. She dug her nails into his chest, eliciting a groan from him an instant before she shoved, pushing him backward onto the bed. Before he'd stopped bouncing, grinning up at her like he was having the most fun of his life, Ruby followed him, climbing over him and crawling upward until she straddled his hips.

She might have taken things further, sliding her drenched pussy along the ridge of his cock, if Liam hadn't chosen right then to distract her. He cupped her breasts from behind, plumping them and pressing them together as he talked to Ace as if she wasn't right there between them. "She has amazing tits, doesn't she?"

"Just the right size. And those pink nipples..." Ace reached for them, but Liam smacked his hands away.

"Mine," Liam chastised. "You play with her pussy."

"Using my dick?" Ace asked with a lopsided grin that stole her breath. He was handsome, yes, but his expression reminded her so much of the less mature, goofy guy who never hesitated to watch cartoons with her while curled up on matching bean bags in the Shields' lounge.

That smile and his easy joy in simple pleasures had been missing lately. If she could bring it back, she would. Especially if all it took was letting him fuck the shit out of her. Win-win.

"Fingers first. Don't rush her." Liam took Ace's hand and guided it to her core. Ace took over, first rubbing around her entrance then across it, accustoming her to his touch before he slipped a digit inside her. And when he did, Liam was there, murmuring reassurances in her ear even as he raked his teeth down the column of her neck.

Ace's fingers stretched her, making her wonder how she'd ever take his dick, never mind Liam's, which was as girthy as his barrel chest and tree-trunk thighs had led her to assume when she'd pictured him nude in her imagination.

She arched in his hold, trying to align her skin with his mouth. He sucked a spot immediately below her ear. The combination of the pressure of his lips and the scratch of his beard made her cry out. Ace froze, his fingers embedded in the entrance of her pussy.

"You're not hurting her," Liam promised.

"Not at all." Ruby sank lower over his hand, impaling herself on it.

"Fuck, you're so hot. And wet." Ace continued working his hand into her, rubbing her in places she hadn't known could feel that good. He curled his fingers within her, making her shudder in Liam's grip. Liam wasn't about to let her fall and instead continued to distract her from any mild discomfort by pinching her nipples and raking his teeth along the column of her neck.

They might have done this often, but she certainly had no stamina built up. "Guys. I... That feels..."

She couldn't tell them that they were in danger of finishing their fun before they'd started.

"Are you saying you're about to come already?" Liam didn't seem as upset by the idea as she was.

Her cheeks flamed and not only from desire.

"That's good, Ruby." Ace added his thumb to the action, strumming slow circles around her clit as he pumped his fingers in and out of her. "We'll give you plenty of orgasms if you'll let us."

Her panicked gaze winged to Liam's.

His eyes widened as he studied her up close. "How much experience do you have, Ruby?"

Held tight in his arms and impaled on Ace's hands, she didn't want to admit the truth lest they find her less desirable for it. But Liam wasn't about to let her get away with avoiding him. "How many times has a man made you come before?"

"Once," she whispered, thinking of the night before when they'd done such a good job of it together.

"Once in a whole night?" Ace grumbled. "Fucking idiots."

"Uh..."

"What aren't you saying?" Liam growled. "Tell me or I'll make him stop and I'll put you over my knee until you do."

She wasn't entirely opposed to that plan, but she figured it was best to be honest considering she wanted a lot more from them than a single afternoon in bed. "Once. Ever. You guys."

Liam froze then too. His arm banded around her, keeping her tight to him. "You're not telling me you're a virgin."

"Not exactly." She shook her head. "I let my lab partner fuck me in college to see what the fuss was about, but wasn't impressed enough for a repeat performance. Plus last night counts for something, right?"

"It counted for a lot," Ace told her, always free with his emotions. Then his brows knit. "But…"

"That asshole who took your virginity didn't even make sure you enjoyed it, did he?" Liam's eyes were gorgeous this close and his stare speared straight into her soul.

She shook her head no.

"We're about to make up for that," Liam promised her.

"Should I slow down?" Ace asked Liam, relying on his partner to think things through when he so often acted on impulse.

"Does it look like she's not ready?" Liam shot back. "Does it feel like she needs you to hold out on her?"

Ruby whimpered at that thought alone. She squirmed, trying to force Ace deeper within her.

"Make her explode on your fingers, Ace, then you can show her what a real man does with his dick." Liam held her, cradling her against his mammoth chest as Ace did exactly that.

Ruby gasped when he shifted, his fingers reaching deep within her. He moved them, pressing against someplace sensitive before spreading them open and stretching her. All the while his thumb kept up its relentless rubbing. She dropped her head back onto Liam's shoulder as he kept her upright, and when he tipped his head over hers and sealed their mouths in their first ever kiss—rough, raw, and passionate—she lost control.

Her entire body spasmed, her pussy hugging Ace's fingers even as Liam swallowed her moans. They were experts in bed, able to play her body like she could get code to sing for her. They knew exactly where and how to touch her to enhance the sensations flooding her. And when the peak had passed and she turned limp, Liam waited for Ace to withdraw his hand, then laid her in Ace's welcoming arms.

Ace was sweet and free with his affection as he told her how amazing she was and how he'd loved feeling her body respond to his touch.

But it was when Liam grabbed Ace's wrist and lifted Ace's fingers to his own lips that Ruby realized one orgasm wasn't going to cut it. As he sucked on Ace's index and middle fingers, Ace's cock throbbed against her pussy and rekindled her arousal.

"Too soon?" Ace asked Liam, his voice sounding raspier than she'd ever heard it.

"Up to her." Liam arranged her hair off to one side so he could stroke her back from shoulders to her ass. "You've waited long enough to have him inside you, haven't you?"

"Too long." Ruby levered herself up, planting her palms on Ace's chest. She hoped he realized she wasn't only talking about that afternoon.

"Let me help you." Liam took her hips in his hands and lifted, directing her uncoordinated limbs, still tingling with pleasure. When he raised her, Ace fisted the base of his cock and angled it upward, aiming it at her pussy.

Ruby had never imagined she'd have not only one but two incredible men to make all her fantasies come true.

But now that she was there, between them, she couldn't deny that Liam's clear thoughts and steady guidance made things better for both her and Ace, and hopefully him too.

She was able to relax and let go of the anxiety that sometimes kept her brain in hyper mode. Liam would make sure Ace enjoyed himself too, which was a huge weight off her mind that allowed her to simply experience instead of fixating on the details and whether or not she was doing it right. Whatever that meant.

They were perfect for her in every way. Not the least of which being how Ace filled her. Because just then, the tip of his cock notched at the entrance to her body.

Except Liam wouldn't lower her onto his partner's shaft no matter how she tried to force their connection. "Shit, Ruby. I didn't ask about protection."

It had slipped her mind, but not his. He would always look out for her.

"I'm on birth control and healthy. I have to take the same physicals as the rest of the team for some dumb reason." She rolled her eyes at Jordan's rules, though at the moment, she didn't mind so much.

"So are we," Ace told her.

"Then let me have him," Ruby demanded of Liam.

"Bossy." He nipped the tip of her nose. "Fine. But only because I can't wait to see his cock spreading that pretty pussy wide and getting you ready for mine."

Well, that did it. Ruby could have sworn she got wetter with every word he spoke, drenching Ace's cock and allowing her body to slide down it effortlessly when Liam lowered her inch by inch.

Ace's warm eyes slammed shut and he pounded the bed on either side of her legs. "Oh fuck. That feels so good. I always knew you'd be amazing wrapped around my dick."

"Does it hurt at all? Don't lie." Liam drew her attention back to him with a twist to one of her nipples. If that was the kind of pain he meant, the pleasurable sort, she wouldn't have cared even if it had, but it didn't.

"No. Incredible." More than that was beyond her.

Ruby wanted to ride Ace, but without muscle memory to guide her, she relied on Liam to set the pace and limits of her movements. He essentially used her like a living toy to fuck his boyfriend.

That thought did nothing to dampen the arousal growing within her again.

"Can you take him a little deeper?" Liam asked, nipping her jaw. "You have almost all of him now."

There was more? Ruby moaned. "Yes. Give him to me. Please."

She met Ace's gaze as Liam settled her fully onto Ace's torso. They stared into each other's eyes as they were fused entirely for the first time. Of many, she hoped. His head thrashed on the bed, his short hair ruffling as his abdomen flexed. She felt his dick jerk inside her, setting off another round of pleasurable waves.

Liam carefully peeled his hands from her, letting her have free rein. "Go ahead, Ruby. Ride him. Rub your clit on his body and grind on his cock until you come again."

"You're not going to help me?" She peeked over her shoulder at him worriedly.

"You've got this. Listen to your instincts." Liam petted her ass, then smacked it lightly. "I'll be right here if you need me."

Ruby nodded and began to move, finding the rhythm that set off the most fireworks in her veins fairly quickly.

She focused on repeating the motion, as Ace put his hands on her waist and steadied her.

"There you go. Good girl," Liam coached as he stood back to watch. His hand fisted his own cock, which looked painfully erect. When he lifted it, she got a better look at the series of piercings that formed a ladder along the underside of his shaft. He caught her staring and smiled slowly. "Do you like that?"

She nodded. "What does it feel like?"

Ace answered for her, sweat starting to dot his brow as he plowed up into her from below even as she ground down onto him. "It's magical. Like someone rubbing you in all the right places."

Ruby moaned.

"You'll find out soon enough," Liam murmured in her ear, making her aware for the first time that she might be into dirty talk. "There's no way you're leaving this bed without my cock buried inside you, fucking you as well as Ace is right now."

She gasped when her muscles clenched around Ace's shaft and squeezed. Liam surprised her when he caught her hair in his fist, close to the base of her neck, and used the grip to press her down until her chest tucked against Ace's. He angled her head so that her lips were close to his lover's, practically daring her to kiss the other man.

So she did. And nearly bit him when Liam traced the rim of her pussy around Ace's embedded cock. When Ace grunted into her parted lips, Liam took that as an invitation. He tunneled into her, his finger running along the prominent vein on the underside of Ace's shaft. The thought that it could someday be his cock, stretching her impossibly so she could hold them both together, turned Ruby on so much she smothered his hand, only increasing the pressure on Ace's dick, and his self-control.

He kissed her almost desperately, all hints of playfulness vanished.

It could have been he was imagining the same thing as Ruby. Liam certainly was. "Someday, after we stretch you open, you're going to have us both. Here. Together."

"Oh!" Ruby had heard Kennedy, Sola, Laurel, and James swapping stories of some of the sexual gymnastics they'd undertaken with their partners. But until that moment, Ruby realized she hadn't truly comprehended the depth of wonder two—or more—lovers could bring to the equation. Their effect on her was more than doubled. They magnified each other's efforts, creating an exponential benefit for her.

Now that Liam had reinforced the idea in her mind, she wished he'd deliver on his promise. Right then.

But he knew, even if she didn't in that moment, that she wasn't ready for that yet.

Liam kept them focused on the pleasure they were bringing each other right then. Ace stuttered beneath her, then cursed when she backed off long enough to realize what was happening.

When she glanced over her shoulder, she glimpsed Liam toying with Ace's balls, tugging on them harder than she would have thought would be entirely pleasurable, though Ace didn't seem to mind. He propped his feet flat on the bed and dropped his knees wide open, giving Liam room to work.

At the same time, Liam snaked one hand around her waist and arrowed in on her clit as though he knew she needed some help concentrating on the storm of ecstasy brewing within her with so many sensual distractions surrounding her.

Ruby's body began to gather again, and she redoubled her efforts, working her pussy over Ace's shaft even as he rocked upward, bottoming out inside her.

"Fuck, Liam. You better quit that if you want me to last." Ace sounded tortured in all the best ways. "It's hard enough when I finally have you both. Here with me."

He seemed like he was teetering on the edge when he groaned that last part. Ruby clung to him, prepared to kiss the shit out of him again until Liam slid onto the bed beside them and gave Ace something better to do with his mouth.

He used two fingers on top of his shaft to press it down and tap it against Ace's parted lips several times before fitting the fat head to Ace's mouth. Ruby reached out before she realized she intended to and fingered the jewelry in his thick shaft.

Liam cursed and stared at the ceiling as if the sight of her hand on his cock and Ace's mouth about to swallow him whole were too much to take in at once.

"You know if I taste you while I'm fucking her, I don't stand a chance, right?" Ace looked worried as he stared up at Liam.

The bigger guy returned his attention to them, brushing Ace's hair off his forehead. He grinned bit wickedly then. "That's my plan. When she comes again, I want you to fill her up. Shoot deep in that pussy so that when I'm in there next, I can feel the mess you've left behind all over my cock."

"Son of a bitch." Ace scrunched his eyes closed.

Ruby was no less affected. Her thighs already quaked as

she rubbed herself full-length along Ace, taking pleasure from every bit of him within and against her. Liam had to hurry. She quit playing with his piercings and guided his cock into Ace's mouth, feeding Ace his partner's cock.

Ace's jaw nearly unhinged to take the whole thing and the sight of him trying desperately to swallow Liam's shaft had her teetering on the verge of another climax.

Liam didn't hold back. He gave them both what they wanted, fucking Ace's mouth as Ace's neck strained upward to take even more. He gripped the back of Ace's head and pumped with short, careful strokes. At the same time, he leaned toward Ruby. He used her shoulder to raise her so that he could kiss her. When their mouths collided, they formed a triangle. Her mouth and his connected as did her and Ace's groins. Ace's mouth around Liam's shaft completed the arrangement.

To be joined with them in an endless loop of desire set something off in Ruby. She cried out between Liam's lips, loving the way he took control of their making out and their fucking. He set the pace and Ace followed, pistoning upward into Ruby in time to Liam's own thrusts into Ace's throat.

Ace must have been practically suffocated by them, but he didn't seem to mind.

Liam opened his eyes and locked his stare on hers as if giving her some kind of warning. If it was supposed to be about Ace losing control, he shouldn't have bothered because she was right there with him.

Ruby screamed into his mouth as she shattered, her body undulating around Ace double time when Liam palmed her breast and squeezed. She tore her lips away to try desperately to draw in a breath and saw Ace multitasking, rolling Liam's balls around in his palm. That did nothing to subdue her rapture.

She came so hard she thought she might break Ace, but his moans didn't sound like painful ones when he froze then went into a flurry of movement, swallowing around Liam and pounding into her, extending the waves of pleasure battering her nerve endings.

"Yes. Come hard," Liam barked to Ace, squeezing his shoulder. "Flood that pussy and show her how good it feels to be buried inside her."

Ruby had never been as satisfied as when Ace did just that. He pumped her full of jet after jet of his release, leaving her no doubt about how well she'd pleased him despite her lack of experience.

Her gaze shot to Liam's then, desperate, hoping he knew what she needed because she felt like she was on fire and nothing was ever going to put it out. She was falling and needy and lost. Ruby stared up at him. "Help me."

He sprang into action then, carefully removing his dick from Ace's still suckling mouth to avoid hitting his piercings on the other man's teeth.

Liam wasn't gentle or playful like Ace. He was deliberate and sure and so damn commanding there was no sense in resisting. He pulled her off of Ace with a wet pop that made both her and Ace groan and continue to shiver.

"I hope you didn't think you were done," he rumbled in her ear before shoving her face-down against the mattress and raising her hips. He smacked her ass hard enough that the shockwave penetrated her sex-hazed mind.

Even Ace began to rouse. His voice was a little

concerned when he realized what was happening. "Liam..."

"No. This is what you two wanted and now you're going to get it." A side of Liam she realized he kept carefully buried began to emerge. Ruby flung her hand out and Ace caught it as he rolled onto his side next to her. He stared into her eyes, assessing her emotions.

It wasn't panic he'd see there, but anticipation. And hope.

Ace kissed the tip of her nose. "I'm right here. Tell me if it's too much. I'll take him for you."

Ruby whimpered when a trickle of fluid slipped from her, but if anything it seemed to only turn Liam on more. He pounced on her, burying his face against her pussy and licking the proof of Ace's possession from her wrecked flesh.

She couldn't tell if she was still coming or he was spiraling her upward again with his mouth on her, but by the time he finished lapping Ace's come from her pussy and paused to bite her ass cheek, she didn't care. "Liam. More."

"You want my cock?" He knelt behind her, the weight of his shaft spreading her cheeks so she could discern its thickness and heft clearly.

"Shit, you look huge next to her." Ace had perked up and was paying full attention.

Ruby didn't realize she hadn't answered until Liam began tapping her pussy with the blunt head of his erection. "Say it, Ruby. Tell me you want this in you, spreading you wide."

"I do." She rocked backward, but he wasn't the sort of man to be bullied. He smacked her ass again, warming it with his aggressive touch. "Fuck me, Liam. Please."

Ace groaned as Liam's cock began to sink inside her. It burned some, and she was thankful that Ace's come was there to slick her even more than her arousal alone. Liam fit an inch into her and then a couple. And when the first bead of the barbells on his piercing slipped into her pussy, rubbing against the front wall of it, she swore she blacked out for a second.

"She's fine, Liam. She loves it," Ace was promising his lover. *Their* lover. "Give her more. Give her all of you."

Ruby knew from his wistful tone that was everything Ace had wanted from the other man. All of him. Much more than simply his cock. At least that was a place to start.

She clawed at the sheets. "Don't hold back now."

"You have no idea what you're asking for." Liam growled as he hunched over her back, drilling deeper and adding even more sparkles of sensation with each of his piercings that prodded against her.

"It's okay. *She's* okay." Ace comforted them both, rubbing Ruby's shoulder and petting Liam's abs. Was this how he was with Ace? Always afraid of being *too much* the same as Ruby often was in other ways. She would think about that later, when her brain was functioning again.

Liam let out a noise that was half strangled moan and half roar. He plunged the rest of the way into her with a single powerful thrust that shoved her several inches up the bed. Ace braced her, keeping her steady as Liam began to fuck.

He put one hand on her hip for leverage and the other wrapped around her throat.

Ruby swore she came right then or maybe it was an aftershock from the orgasm Ace had given her, but either way, her body bucked beneath Liam. He leaned on her, his weight pinning her in place as he drove into her, his hips slapping her ass with every stroke.

Her pussy was so full she swore he'd stuffed every available bit of it with him and those relentless metal balls that massaged her perfectly.

"You're doing great, Ruby. Taking him like that." Ace seemed in awe of her when all she was doing was flying in their arms.

Her breasts hung heavy beneath her, swaying with each of Liam's strokes. And when she shifted to alleviate some of the pressure, Ace realized what was distracting her. He reached beneath her, playing with them, keeping them from swinging as violently and turning the sensation into something entirely pleasurable.

Too damn good.

She had no warning. Another wave of pleasure crested over her, making her shriek and tremble beneath Liam's unrelenting fucking. This time it was too much, his cock and his piercings rasping against her ultra-sensitive flesh.

Ruby's gaze flew to Ace's, her eyes wide.

"Hold on, Liam." Ace put his hand on Liam's pelvis and stilled him. "She's tapped out."

Liam instantly withdrew, a little more sharply than she might have preferred, leaving her shockingly empty. Ruby gasped, trying to catch her breath as rapture swamped her. Still there was a hint of regret. She tried to object. "No. Not yet. I can take more. He hasn't come yet."

"This isn't the sort of thing to lie about." Ace leaned in and kissed her gently. "It's fine. I told you, I've got you covered."

He helped Ruby settle herself on her back, utterly spent, propped up on Liam's pillows so she had a perfect view when Liam gripped Ace's hair in one fist and dragged the other man toward him. He was incredible, kneeling over them, his broad chest and honed physique glistening with a sheen of perspiration. He could easily have been an ancient god of love or war.

Maybe both.

Ace went willingly when Liam directed his face toward his sloppy cock, coated in a mixture of Ruby's arousal and Ace's own come. Ace didn't hesitate, lapping their mingled fluids from Liam's nearly purple shaft, which was harder than could possibly be comfortable.

His piercings stood out now against his straining flesh, making her whimper as she remembered the delicious things they'd done to her insides.

Ace cleaned Liam, then looked up, a puzzled expression coming over his face before he pulled back. "You're not going to fuck me? After all that, you're going to settle for a blow job?"

Ruby immediately sensed a shift in the room. Things got tense, and not the good kind either.

"Your mouth is plenty for me." Liam cupped Ace's cheek in his hand. "I was losing control. Too rough with her and with you..."

He shook his head.

"You don't think I can take it?" Ace's jaw tightened. "That I can't handle you anymore? You've fucked me plenty since my accident. Or is it because of today? How I couldn't take that shot?"

Oh no. They were not going to ruin the moment. Not when she was enjoying it so thoroughly they'd ensured she'd never be satisfied with anyone else.

"No one thinks that, Ace." Ruby glared at Liam, daring him to fuck things up. She would do things to that spectacular cock of his that were entirely unpleasant if he cut Ace right then, where he was most vulnerable.

"He does." Ace started to back away, but Ruby wrapped her hand around his wrist, keeping him there with them.

"And fucking you like I was just doing to her is going to prove you're wrong?"

"It's a place to start." Ace looked up at the ceiling then back to Liam, putting his bravery on full display. "But no, not fucking me like you were fucking her. You were still being reserved. I'm not new to this. I know what I'm asking for and I want everything. All you have to give. So come on, Liam. Fuck me. Hard. Rough. And without hedging, if you really mean it."

There was something in the defensive set of Ace's shoulders that made Ruby certain he didn't think Liam was going to take him up on his offer.

But then Liam looked to her. She nodded.

And he went for it.

12

———

Ace blinked. He couldn't believe it. Liam had reached his limit, that place where he freaked out and had always turned back before. Except for the first time in their relationship, with Ruby there—or maybe because of how things had gone that morning—Liam wasn't running, unless it was toward them instead of in the opposite direction.

The disappointment he'd braced himself against vanished as Liam shook his head and leaned closer. "This is probably the stupidest thing I've ever done. But first you, then JRad, and now Ruby..."

"Trust us." Ruby sat up and clutched Liam's hand. "I know you're trying to do the right thing, to protect us, but shutting us out isn't working. Don't mistreat him anymore, Liam. Please."

"Are you begging me to fuck the shit out of your boyfriend right now?" Liam looked at her with a glint in his eyes and the start of a wicked grin that would have melted Ace's underwear off if he'd been wearing any.

"Yeah." Ruby pleaded their case. "Give him what he

needs, like you did for me. I'm here. I'll watch him, like he took care of me. I'll make sure that he's safe even if you get carried away in the moment."

Liam took a huge breath then let it out in a shaky exhalation. His cock bobbed between his legs, still painfully hard, clearly in favor of Ruby's plan.

Ace didn't wait. He assumed her position, kneeling, his face resting on her abdomen and his ass in the air, knees spread wide and his rapidly re-hardening cock clearly displayed for Liam. Ruby's fingers stroked his hair. She massaged his head until he hummed and nuzzled against her. Sex mixed with the light citrus of her body wash formed a scent uniquely theirs. One he'd never forget.

This was where he was meant to be. Caught between them. And now he only needed Liam to believe it too. To step up and take control instead of being too decent to assume command for longer than it took to dole out a few orgasms.

Liam retrieved a bottle of lube from a nearby dresser drawer. The gel was cool against Ace's asshole, but the heat of Liam's fingers chased it away. He clenched his jaw and closed his eyes, willing to take whatever Liam would give him and be grateful to be one step closer to his ultimate fantasy, but Ruby—damn her—noticed and called him out.

"Something's not right," Ruby told Liam, living up to her promise.

"What?" Liam hesitated. "Have you changed your mind, Ace?"

He shook his head, rubbing his cheek on Ruby's torso. Did he dare be greedy enough to ask?

Liam slapped his ass, hard. "Tell me or I'm going to go take a cold shower right fucking now."

Not the goddamn showers again. Besides, even if it was ice water, nothing had the power to deflate Liam's massive hard-on except an epic orgasm. "Fuck. Fine. I want you to tie me up."

It had been months...

"Your arm—"

"Kennedy said it's fine," Ace blurted as he glanced over his shoulder.

"You asked her if it was okay to be restrained while I fuck you senseless?" Liam tipped his head.

"Not in those exact words, but yes." He winced, his own cock deflating some.

What if Liam still wouldn't do it? What if he thought of Ace as less capable of handling him since his injury no matter how much he protested when Ace brought it up? "She said as long as it's not twisted behind my back and it's not bearing my weight, it's okay. She also recommended wide cuffs instead of bare rope or some other pervertable lying around."

"Then let's wait until I can order—"

"They're in my room. In the drawer of my nightstand." Ace's dick rebounded, leaking some as he thought of how he'd worn them at night when jacking off while Liam took so many of his now-infamous showers.

"Oooh, can I see?" Ruby perked up. "Would they fit me too or are they too big?"

Ace couldn't help but laugh. Of course she wouldn't think less of him for it. And yeah, they'd work just fine if she ever wanted to find out what it was like. He'd be more than happy to show her. "They're adjustable."

"Sweet." She grinned.

"You two are going to be the death of me." Liam

pointed to Ruby. "Will you get them while I finish prepping him?"

She nodded eagerly, then kissed Ace before squirming out from beneath him and scurrying toward his room. Could she really be into watching Liam top him? It seemed so.

"Fuck, we're the luckiest bastards alive," Liam muttered as he ringed Ace's hole. But before Ace could wholeheartedly agree, Liam slipped two fingers inside of him. Given the plugs he'd gotten in the habit of wearing to bed and around the apartment in order to be ready for Liam whenever the other guy caved and gave into his cravings for intimacy, Liam's digits entered him smoothly. "You've been playing with your toys again, haven't you?"

"You didn't leave me a lot of choice." Ace hated the pouty tone of his accusation, but it was true.

"I'm sorry, Ace." Liam bent down and kissed his back all along his spine. That unusually tender display did more to turn him on than Liam's hand buried within him. "The truth is I'm nowhere near as brave as you."

"You can make it up to me now." Ace groaned as Liam fed him another finger.

"I'll do my best," Liam promised before exploring deeper, then curling his fingers. When he stroked near Ace's prostate, a spurt of precome dripped to the bed beneath them.

Even half-assed from Liam was spectacular. Ace might not survive a proper effort, especially with Ruby there to play with him. But at least it was a hell of a lot better way to go than on an assignment gone wrong.

Ruby dashed into the room and cannonballed onto the bed beside him. The metal D-rings on the leather cuffs jingled in her grasp.

"Oof." Liam grunted as he steadied them on the wobbling mattress.

Ace grinned up at her, as eager as she obviously was for the show they were about to put on. Any misgivings he'd had about what she would think of him for submitting to Liam vanished when he saw how into it she was. "I'm glad you like this."

"Are you kidding?" She lifted his face even as she twisted herself into a human pretzel, cross-legged and bent in half so that she could kiss him. "I've been dying to watch you fuck and finally see what I've only heard all those times before."

Oh. Right. He'd forgotten about that.

"I bet it's even hotter than I imagined." Ruby sighed. Ace wished he could go back and change so many things. But all he could do was live in the moment and enjoy. Their careers and the atrocities they'd seen while doing their jobs had impressed on him the importance of not wasting opportunities.

"Give me a hand, Ruby." Liam used his chin to gesture to his headboard. "Clip those to the metal loops on each post of the bed."

Her gaze flew to the discreet details in the metalworking. "You dirty boys. I love it."

She inspected the cuffs, then fastened them where Liam had indicated. Somehow, having her involved only made Ace more excited for what was to come. He liked them teaming up on him.

"Yank on them. Make sure they're secure," Liam directed as he spread his fingers, stretching Ace's hole plenty to ensure that even his fat dick wouldn't be a problem for Ace to take comfortably.

Ruby did, and when they were both satisfied, Liam

shocked Ace by withdrawing quickly and grabbing his hips. Before he knew it, he was flipping, tumbling to his back on the bed as Liam and Ruby hovered over him, their gazes hungry and expectant.

"You get his good arm." Liam took Ace's hand and gave it to Ruby. She squeezed his fingers before stretching his arm toward the cuff. Ace let her do whatever she pleased with him, a zing running from her fingers through his entire body to his balls when the fuzzy insides of the cuff encircled his wrist. "Strap him in so he can't get away. But not too tight. We don't want to cut off his circulation. Make sure you can slip a finger or two between the leather and his skin."

Ace was pretty sure from the knowing grin Liam flashed him that he was letting Ruby have her fun primarily to turn Ace on even more. And it was working.

With his free hand, he reached for his dick to stroke it a bit and relieve some of the ache there. But Liam intercepted it before he could fist himself. "Uh uh. None of that. Only we get to play with your cock now."

Liam captured his other wrist and carefully brought it toward the open, waiting cuff. When he was nearly there, Liam asked, "How's this? Not stretching it too much?"

"It's fine." Ace needed him to hurry but there was no use.

"If I find out you're lying to me, the spanking you get will not be the fun kind." Liam leaned down and nipped his ear. "Tell me the truth."

"It's a little uncomfortable, but nothing I can't handle." And that was honest. In fact it felt better than when he'd been on all fours, leaning on his folded arms.

Liam stroked the scarred area around his fucked up tattoos and the pocked skin and muscle. Ace tried to withdraw then, ashamed of the imperfections, but Liam wouldn't allow him to hide. He made quick work of buckling Ace into the cuff, then rubbed the area around the healed wound, massaging it as he had so often during Ace's rehab.

"You swear you'll let Ruby and me know if it hurts, even a little?" Liam looked as if he would bolt unless Ace promised.

So he nodded vehemently. "Yeah. But right now it's not my arm that's the problem."

Ace lifted his pelvis, thrusting his rock-hard cock in the air.

Ruby licked her lips as she admired it. Was she getting turned on again now that she'd had a small reprieve? He could take care of that.

Liam must have noticed her subconscious gesture. He reached across Ace and clasped her waist. With hardly any effort, he lifted her and put her where he wanted: straddling Ace's shoulders. Her pussy was barely out of reach, though Ace automatically strained his neck to try to lick her glistening folds, slick with her arousal and his own earlier release.

Next Liam took Ace's ankles, one in each of his massive hands, and lifted them until he could hand them to Ruby, bending Ace practically in half.

"Now?" Liam asked.

With his ass exposed and his cock lying stiff on his torso, Ace squirmed in an attempt to get closer to Ruby, Liam, or both. The pressure on his arm was the least of his concerns. "My arm is fine. My dick is not. Come on, Liam. I'm suffering when you hold out on me. Give me what I need. Everything this time. All of you."

Ruby gasped, her fingers tightening on his ankles, which only made him hornier.

Liam bowed his head for a second. There was no way he would back out now, was there?

Ace swore time froze.

Then Liam lifted his face toward Ace and Ruby and groaned. "I couldn't stop even if I wanted to. God help me."

He stepped onto the bed and knelt near Ace's prominently displayed ass. Then he was lubing not only Ace's open hole but his own cock. He made sure to coat the underside of his shaft and his jewelry there despite the fact that he wore smooth small-gauge barbells that had never felt anything but incredible in Ace's ass.

Liam knelt, towering over both Ace and Ruby as he stroked himself, his gorgeous pierced cock stiffer than Ace could ever remember it being before. And when he fit the wide head of it to Ace's hole, they both moaned.

"Yup. That's what it sounded like," Ruby teased, though not for long.

"When I bury myself in him, you're going to lower yourself. I want you to ride his fucking face. Rub that pussy on it. Soak him. Make him lick his come out of it and taste how good you are together." Liam advanced at that last bit, as if Ruby and Ace together tested his legendary self-control. Ace's mouth opened on a gasp and was quickly filled with the sweet flesh of Ruby's pussy.

For a moment he was afraid he'd actually died on their mission that morning and gone to heaven. Because surely, this was what it was for him.

He kissed Ruby, hoping she knew how much she was changing things between Liam and him. How much she was making possible by bridging the gap between them.

She held Ace open for Liam, who embedded his cock slowly, one piercing at a time, to give Ace a chance to adjust.

None of his toys were as big as his partner, nor as warm.

Damn.

Ace's cock twitched, spilling more precome, which pooled on his abdomen.

Ruby moaned. "Damn, that's so sexy. You two are so gorgeous together."

Ace tugged at his bonds then, wishing he could touch her but thrilled when he remembered why he couldn't. He wished they'd never let him go and keep him there as their pet fuckboy for the rest of his life.

Then it became difficult to think at all because Liam began to screw him. With long, slow strokes at first that devolved into a frenzied fucking. He was rougher than he'd ever been before, thrilling Ace and reassuring him that Liam might not think he was weak and damaged after all.

When Ace stiffened at that, Ruby lifted herself up and sat back. She petted his face, wiping it clean when she asked, "Are you okay? How's your arm?"

"Fine. It's fine. I'm fine. Don't stop."

"You're sure?" She peered into his eyes as Liam kept pounding into him. Ace's ass clenched Liam's dick when it seemed like he might withdraw.

"I swear." More than that would have been impossible to say.

Ruby looked over at Liam and nodded. "He's good. Keep going."

Liam tossed back his head, the golden strands of his hair and beard glinting in the late afternoon sunlight.

Then he caught Ace off guard by dropping in close, grinding against him as his hands went to Ace's neck. He put some pressure there, though not enough to do any damage, in a possessive grip that Ace had never dared to dream of asking for. When he did, Ruby's pussy slid over his wrist, the sinew of his arm giving her clit something to rub against.

She cried out and so did Ace, which must have only enhanced the sensation on her pussy.

Ruby called his name then Liam's before shuddering above him. There was no doubt she was coming when her pussy clenched and another wave of wetness burst across his tongue. Knowing she was enjoying this as much as he was...or at least enough to orgasm...drove him wild.

"Someone touch my cock. Please." Ace writhed between them. The bonds at his wrists, Ruby's hands ringing his ankles and the pressure of Liam's broad chest on the back of his thighs all combining to make him feel secure and wanted and...theirs.

"Do you really think that's a good idea?" Liam asked in a ragged voice. "Or are you going to come all over yourself and end our fun before we're finished with you?"

"I'll tell you if I'm too close," Ace promised despite the sweet torture it would be if they left him hanging. All he cared about was getting them to touch him.

Ruby made soft noises as her climax receded, but she didn't back off.

"We're going to wait for her to join us," Liam told Ace.

"I'm good. Seriously." Ruby sounded dazed. "Incredible."

"You have one more in you," Liam insisted.

"I do?" She sounded skeptical, but her pussy spasmed on Ace's tongue.

"Yeah." Liam grunted as he drove inside Ace with a particularly bold thrust. Something about either their position or his lover's extra vigor made Liam's piercings caress Ace particularly effectively. He groaned.

"Play with him if you need some inspiration. Look at his cock. How long it is and how hard. That's for you, Ruby, you know that, right? He loved fucking you." Liam's dirty talk was no lie. Ace had enjoyed every second inside her and couldn't wait to do it again sometime soon. "He loves being smothered by your wet pussy."

Also true.

"Go ahead. I've got his legs. Jack him off. But if I tell you to stop, let go right away," Liam warned.

"Okay." Ruby sounded awed as she transferred his ankles to Liam's much stronger grasp, then planted one hand on his tensed abs. Her fingertip drew circles through the slickness there, getting her hand lubed before she curled it around him.

He almost shot right then.

Liam slammed balls-deep into Ace and froze, giving him a second to adjust to their multi-pronged attack on his senses. His piercings glided in small circles as he ground his hips against Ace's ass instead of fucking.

"Like this?" Ruby asked, her innocence peeking through.

So Ace groaned, trying to tell her as best he could how fantastic she made him feel. Whenever she did something that felt particularly good, he made sure to suck her clit and give her feedback even if speaking was beyond him.

Liam resumed his fucking in time to Ruby's strokes. It didn't take very long before Ace felt himself gathering around Liam and his cock straining in Ruby's grasp. He turned his head so he could mumble against Ruby's thigh.

"I'm close," he warned them.

"Stop," Liam ordered Ruby, who let go instantly, as promised.

She seemed disappointed when she said, "But what if I want to see him come for us? Can I watch him shoot all over his chest when you lose it in his ass?"

"Not helping." Ace groaned and writhed beneath them. Liam chuckled, his own cock throbbing in Ace's ass.

"I have a better idea. Or at least I think so." Liam leaned in, increasing the pressure on Ace's legs, and must have kissed Ruby because she hummed.

"What?" she wondered.

"Why don't you join me over here and fuck him with me? Let him fill that pussy again so the three of us come together." Liam's ragged breathing made it clear the end was nearing. Ace was torn between anticipation of what he knew would be the best orgasm of his life and ending the sharing he'd dreamed of for so long.

"Oh. Okay." Ruby carefully extricated herself from her spot over his face.

"Keep those legs up," Liam barked at Ace before reaching for her. He lifted Ruby and turned her so her back was plastered to Liam's front, then lowered her into place. This time when she tipped his cock up and Liam lowered her onto it, he slid inside her easily.

She reached for Ace's calves, leaning on them for support even as she helped keep him spread wide for Liam, who began to rock once more. It was impossible not to fuck when they were surrounded by Ruby and each other.

As much as Ace had enjoyed feasting on Ruby, he loved watching his two lovers enjoying his body even more. Liam's arm banded around her waist, pinning her to him so that as he fucked into Ace he pulled her off the other guy's cock and when he retreated, he drove her onto Ace's shaft again, burying him deep.

Ruby flung her head back onto Liam's shoulder and bit his neck, which only riled him more. Liam pounded Ace's ass and used Ruby to fuck his cock at the same time.

Liam snuck his free hand around her hip to rub her clit.

Their motions were jerky and a little clumsy though powerful. The three of them took each other to an impossible high, too aroused to stop or care about perfection. They strained together toward the perfect finish.

Ace was about to tell them he needed another break when Ruby shattered. She screamed loud enough that it could probably be heard thorough the entire building and not only next door. Liam kept her moving, gloving Ace's erection with her clenching pussy. Ace was lost. He strained against his bonds and pressed his ass tight to Liam, who was drilling him into the mattress.

The instant he came, flooding Ruby's pussy and drawing on Liam's cock with his ass, Liam roared. He bit Ruby's shoulder as he emptied himself into Ace. Ace forgot to breathe as he milked every last drop from Liam's balls as Ruby's pussy did the same to him.

Nothing had ever felt so right or terrified him as much.

Because now that he knew how great sex, and life in general, could be with both of these people, he refused to settle for less ever again. The climax that rushed through him lingered, wringing every last bit of energy from his muscles until he sagged with the ultimate relief.

It took a while for them to recover from the initial shockwave of their combined passion. But eventually

Liam lowered Ruby to Ace's chest, his legs now sprawled on the bed. She curled up on top of him making happy hums and sighs. Ace kissed her forehead as Liam set him free.

He didn't actually like that part so much except that his arm was starting to ache a bit.

Liam ran his hand over the area that had been shattered, easing the kinks around his elbow. He rubbed it like Kennedy had demonstrated in their physical therapy sessions. "Want your ice pack? Or your brace?"

Ace never wanted to wear that fucking thing again. When he had it on, it was a constant reminder to them all of what had happened. But he would if he needed to. "Thanks, but it's okay for now."

Liam drew a deep breath. "Good. I'm going to go get some washcloths and a different blanket for the bed. Take care of Ruby for me while I'm gone, huh?"

Ace nodded, hugging her tight now that he had use of his arms. She shifted, settling more comfortably against him, her lips brushing the column of his neck. He ran his hands over all of her, from her shoulders down her arms, straightening her hair, caressing her back and ass. He wasn't sure he'd ever met someone who liked to cuddle as much as he did until her.

"Doing okay?" he murmured, kissing her temple.

"Perfect." She smiled up at him. "It was better than I pictured. Way hotter and...so satisfying. I don't want to leave this bed for the next year at least."

She frowned then and he smoothed the lines from between her brows. "What?"

"It's not over. I have to stop those guys." When she shifted, he held her close, selfishly not ready for their intermission from danger to be finished.

"JRad will know if the signal from that drive comes in, yeah?" Damn, she was smart, and adorable, and sexy all in one.

She nodded.

"Then stay. Rest. Be ready for when the team needs you." He didn't say what they both were probably thinking. For when he and Liam needed to go back in the field. And for the time when he would correct the mistake he'd made previously. Hesitation was a thing of the past.

Liam returned then, looking ridiculous draped in a clean comforter that bundled up several of Ruby's plushies and pillows, holding a fistful of washcloths and balancing a tray of drinks and sandwiches in his other arm. He was trying, Ace would give the man that.

Ruby laughed and rolled away to assist. They cleaned up, changed the covers, then climbed back into bed for a picnic together before everything that had transpired that day hit them hard. They probably should have talked about what they'd just done and what it meant that they were about to fall asleep in Liam's bed. But they didn't. It was enough to simply be there, together, for that moment.

And when Liam started snoring softly from where he'd passed out, clearly on his own side of the bed while Ace and Ruby were tangled together in the middle, she peeked up at him from beneath partially lowered lashes.

"Ace?" she whispered.

"Yeah?" He hugged her and her stuffed poop emoji.

"I get it now." She looked away quickly. "Why you held off. I thought it was the worst not knowing if you guys were into me like I wanted you, but now that I know you are, it's scarier thinking he might not plan to ever do more about it than fucking us and pretending like today was only about a bunch of orgasms...even if they were the best ones of my life."

Ace wove his fingers through hers and held her hand tight. He anchored her against his side and promised with his touches and his lazy gaze that he wasn't going anywhere. "Look, I can't speak for him, but you don't have to worry about me, okay?"

She hesitated, then gave a small nod.

"I have feelings for you, Ruby." He kissed her, without any hurry at all. "I wouldn't have slept with you if I didn't. I've always thought you were cute, but it wouldn't be worth the mess—to our careers and our lives here at Shields—if I didn't want more than a convenient fuck every once in a while."

"I've never been so happy to be a hot mess in my life." She snorted against his shoulder.

"That's not what—"

"I know what you meant." She put one finger over his lips before kissing him. "And I feel the same. I...uh...care about you too, Ace. A lot."

She ducked her head then, and he wondered if she could hear his heart racing. She'd given him something Liam never had and maybe never would. Maybe couldn't.

With that, she relaxed against him.

They drifted off together with Liam at least in arms' reach instead of in an entirely different bedroom. It was progress even if it wasn't as much as Ace would have liked.

He tried his best not to be too greedy, especially after he'd been so spoiled.

13

L iam sprawled on one of the obscenely comfortable sectionals in the lounge of the Shields' headquarters. Everyone dealt with the tension of waiting for the hackers to activate Ruby's booby traps in their own way. His arms were spread wide on the back of the cushions. Ace was next to him, tucked into one of the corner spots, while Ruby practically curled up in his lap as they were watching some animated show she was excitedly explaining to him on her tablet.

He had no fucking clue what they were talking about, but they looked cute as fuck huddled together. Nearly as incredible as they'd been snuggled up in his bed that morning.

Liam figured he really should invent some device that applied cold water directly to his junk so he could quit freezing his ass off in the shower. Sure, he'd thought about waking them with his dick in one of their mouths, but he'd used them both thoroughly the night before. Ruby especially had very little practice and he didn't want to push her too far, too fast.

Hell, even with his history, the night before had been *a lot*. He was pretty sure parts of himself he'd never involved before had partaken in their activities. Liam rubbed his chest over his heart.

JRad raised a brow at him, but there was no way Liam could answer his unspoken questions with so many busybodies around. Sola, Aarav, Cash, Marcus, Kennedy, and Knox were playing cards at a table nearby while Jace and Kason worked on their latest song together by the fireplace. Nolan, Wren, and Jordan were the perfect audience for their guys, paying rapt attention to the music they made effortlessly together.

And worst of all...James ambled in with his sister, Laurel, who went directly into Nolan's outstretched arms and perched in his lap. "How'd the pole dancing lesson go?"

"He's sickeningly good at it." Laurel rolled her eyes at her brother. She'd been a pro once, but James was limber and impossibly skilled at harnessing his sexual appeal, none of which should have surprised him given the way he was the centerpiece of the nine-person polyamorous Powertools crew.

"I'm in it for the costumes." James grinned. "I'm ordering these massive sparkly platform heels I found online that will make me like seven feet tall. And I'm thinking of bedazzling a jockstrap to match. I can't wait."

That would be a sight to behold in the Shields' gym, where they had a track, climbing wall, a pool, all the usual weights and gym equipment and now a spinning stripper pole too. To be fair, Liam and Ace had attempted some of the moves and failed spectacularly. The core strength Laurel and James had was impressive.

When Tavish finished skimming through his fitness

magazine and tossed it over Legend, the glossy paper skidded off the surface of the coffee table and onto the floor. James pointed. "Pick that up."

Uh oh. He'd been on a rampage lately. Not that any of them were unnecessarily sloppy, but with their team growing, it was hard to keep things as tidy as they'd once been around headquarters.

Tavish must have had a death wish. He crossed his booted ankles and said, "I thought you were the office manager. Isn't that your job?"

Though he was only kidding, Liam could have told him it wasn't a good idea. JRad grunted from where he and Lucas sat next to them. From the cop that was about as bad as if he'd smacked the other man.

James flipped Tavish the bird. "As good as I would look in that get up, I'll remind you I am *not* your fucking maid. You know what? I think we need a housekeeper, Jordan."

Their boss looked up from where his wife, Wren cuddled in his embrace. Her head rested on his shoulder as she smiled dreamily while she watched Kason singing to her while Jace accompanied him on the blue acoustic guitar that was his prized possession. Jordan agreed. "Yeah, sure. Hire someone."

James took one of the communal tablets from the entertainment center and plopped down on Liam's free side. He started tapping away. Still he glared at Tavish until the guy groaned and peeled himself off the couch that mirrored the one across from it where Liam, Ace, Ruby, and James lounged.

Probably just to get back at them, Tavish made a show of bending over in his kilt, fully mooning James and Liam, who clapped his hand over Ruby's eyes to protect her from Tavish's hairy asshole winking at them. And also because he got a bit jealous thinking of her or Ace looking at other men. Well, shit.

Ruby cracked up along with Ace, and the rest of the Shields. "Guess that answers the question of what you wear under those things."

Liam noticed Legend wasn't laughing, though. He was staring at his roommate, and the private parts he'd exposed, a little too intently to be casual. *Huh.*

"You're lucky I'm not close enough to smack that pasty white ass." James seemed entirely unimpressed. "You need a fucking tan."

"I'll be sure to sunbathe naked this summer for you." Tavish grinned as he set the magazine in its proper place then reclaimed his seat next to Legend.

"Nothing I haven't seen before." James shrugged without looking up from whatever he was doing. "There. I've put an ad on the local job board. Don't fucking scare away our candidates when they come for interviews or you'll be the one on clean-up duty permanently."

"Who's going to be desperate enough to take that job?" Legend chuckled. "We sort of have a reputation around Middletown."

"I made the pay good since they're going to have to put up with all this." James waved his finger around the room. "And threw in room and board because security is important."

Jordan nodded at James.

They probably would have kept talking shit except right then Kason sang a lyric into the lull in the conversation. Jace stopped playing. "No. I think that could be better. What about... And I promise I'll be the dad I never had."

"What'd you say?" James's head cocked, on high alert.

Given that his sister dated Jace and their mutual boyfriend, Nolan, Liam didn't blame him. His jaw went slack and he stared at Laurel.

She waved her hands in front of her chest. "No. I'm not. It's not me."

"Whew. I mean, not that I wouldn't be happy. Ecstatic even. I just... I was surprised, that's all." Nolan put his perfect hair back into place with a swipe of his hand.

Laurel melted against him. "You'd be happy if I was pregnant? Really?"

"Of course." Nolan kissed her forehead and Jace smiled at them both. "If that's what you two wanted."

"Maybe we should call it a night early." Laurel reached for Jace's hand while Nolan held hers.

Now everyone was paying attention. Ace's thigh stiffened against Liam's and Ruby gasped. "Wait, Laurel, you didn't say *nobody's* pregnant. Jace's lyric wasn't metaphorical was it?"

Jace winced as he looked over at Kason. "Sorry I should have kept my mouth shut, but no one ever listens in this place."

"We do when it's good shit." James grinned. "We are super spies, after all."

Kason didn't seem upset. Instead he beamed at Wren and Jordan, who were staring back with equally googly-eyed grins.

"Wren?" Sola asked, setting her cards face down on the table. Kennedy stared at her hands, trying to keep her features schooled when they all were aware of her tell. As their resident doctor, she would be the first to know.

Wow. Instead of looking at Wren, Liam flicked his gaze to Ruby and Ace to see what their reactions were to the news. They stared at each other, equally as sappy as

Jordan and Kason. Did they want a family someday? Did he? That was about a thousand steps beyond where they were but he should ask them sometime.

Assuming they were planning on doing more than sleeping together.

Wren nodded. "I wanted to tell you the other day. But that's when all hell broke loose and it didn't feel like the right time. Jace only knew because he's over every day practicing with Kason and I haven't been feeling so great in the mornings."

"Congratulations!" Laurel leaned in and wrapped Wren in a hug to which the rest of the Shields piled on. They offered their well wishes and chattered excitedly amongst themselves. A baby. That was going to be interesting. The kid would certainly have a lot of uncles and aunts to watch out for it.

Wren peeked at Jordan, who brushed a tear from the corner of her eye and told them all, "If it's a boy, we're going to name him after Johnny."

The wind got sucked out of Liam's chest. Jordan had lived his nightmare. He'd lost his and Wren's partner in a mission gone wrong so many years ago. It had nearly wrecked them, until Kason had brought them back together.

Ace put his hand on Liam's knee and squeezed. When Liam looked at his partner, Ruby was staring between them, frowning. Was she only now realizing what she'd gotten herself into?

"I wouldn't blame you if you didn't want that for yourself," he said quietly so only Ace and Ruby could hear given the din of the rest of their team's celebrations.

Ace grimaced but he nodded. "Having sat here and

waited for Liam to come home the past several months, I know it's not easy."

Wait? What? Had Ace been worried too?

Liam hadn't considered that was part of what had been driving Ace to return to the field so soon. Though he'd be lying if he said he didn't feel better when he knew Ace had his back and he had Ace's. They were damn good partners. In and out of bed.

He might have probed more, but right then Blakely—their practically resident tattoo artist, who was waiting for the Powertools to finish her shop and the secret tunnel beneath it—joined them, swinging her key fob around her index finger. "What's the commotion for?"

"I'm pregnant," Wren answered, her palm next to Jordan's, which rode low on her still-flat belly.

"No kidding!" Blakely crossed to her and gave her a one-armed hug before doing the same to Jordan and Kason. "Congratulations."

Their excitement lingered for a while, though when it died down, Blakely drew Knox over to the couch for the consultation she'd had scheduled with him. He was adding to the back piece he'd started after getting his life together and starting a new one with Kennedy and Marcus.

"Hey, guys, Ruby." Blakely waved as she took out a sketchpad. "How's it going?"

"Pretty damn good." Ruby's face transformed as she smiled.

"That's what we like to hear." Blakely pointed with her pen to Ace's arm. "I see you got your cast off. How's it looking?" He'd already talked to her about the possibility of covering up his scars someday.

"About as shitty as you said it probably would." Ace

grimaced. "I can see why you said you wouldn't touch it for at least six more months."

"Sorry." Blakely crouched at their feet and took Ace's arm in her hands. Ruby leaned closer as if she didn't care for someone else touching her man so intimately. Liam knew how she felt.

Blakely turned it this way and that, then made some notes on her pad. "Yeah, it's raw and you still have healing to do."

Liam shot Ace a look that was mostly, *See? What did I tell you?* But also a little bit of *You're sure I didn't hurt you last night, right?*

Neither of those things seemed to put Ace in a better mood. Liam tried to help. "It won't kill you to wait a bit."

"Oh yeah?" Ace scoffed. "I remember how antsy you were to have your work done. You were trying to get them to do it all at once instead of in sections like they recommended."

James shifted to stare at them. "Liam has a tattoo? Where? I mean, not that I was staring, but I've seen him bare chested and doing squats in those tiny black shorts he works out in."

"I love those shorts." Ruby sighed.

Liam whipped his wide-eyed stare to her. She'd been checking out his ass at the gym? Or maybe his package. Damn.

"They're great. But they don't leave a lot to the imagination." James tapped his chin. "So fess up. What do you have, googly eyes on your balls or what?"

Ace snorted at that, rocking against Liam as he hugged Ruby to him.

"Not a tattoo." Ruby's eyes stared into the distance as if she was recalling memories from the night before. She rambled. "A piercing. No, lots of them. And they're so pretty."

JRad cleared his throat from the opposite sectional. He winked at his protégé. Ruby blinked, then clapped her hand over her mouth, a blush washing her cheeks in the softest pink he'd ever seen. Liam wondered if her ass would turn that same shade if he spanked her for letting his secret out later, not that he really minded.

"Ah hah!" James poked Liam in the chest. "I knew it. You're as kinky as the rest of us. Maybe more. You just hide it better. Those are always the ones you have to look out for."

He stared at Ruby and Ace as he said it. Neither of them denied it. Nor did they look like it bothered them.

"You have a Jacob's ladder?" Blakely asked, her professional curiosity kicking in.

Ruby, ever helpful, said, "It kind of looks like a ladder. Down there, I mean. Yeah."

"They can be tough to get straight." Blakely seemed impressed. "And you need to have a decent amount of real estate to make it look good."

"Oh, that's not a problem," Ace added while he and Ruby grinned at each other. "There are plenty of rungs on it. *Pl-enty.*"

"I'm right fucking here." Liam growled. He knew Ace loved to provoke him because it meant later he'd get the sweetest form of payback. And right then he found he was looking forward to it.

"Okay, I must be dumb. Somebody tell me what we're talking about?" James asked.

Blakely sketched a very unanatomical drawing that looked like a cucumber with dashes through it. "It's a series of frenum piercings. Sometimes with the addition of scrotum rings or a Prince Albert, which goes the other way, up at the tip."

"Damn." James looked at Liam with a newfound respect.

"Do you do those?" Liam asked before he thought better of it. He'd been considering adding one final touch to his collection after reading that they could be particularly pleasurable for his partners.

"Personally, no. But Mike and I designed an in-house piercing area. I have to find the right partner once the city quits screwing with my permits and we can finally open." Blakely sighed. "At least I have you guys to hold me over. You're running out of blank canvases, though."

She turned back to Knox and started flipping to the sketches she'd worked up for him.

James, however, was not so easily diverted. "So, Ruby. When exactly did you see Liam's big fat ladder?"

Ruby choked. Ace patted her on the back as she tried not to swallow her tongue about the time that James's husband and wife strolled in together. They often hung out with him for a while at Shields before the three of them headed to their home at the Powertools complex for the night.

Neil perked up at the talk of construction gear. As a veteran carpenter and now a foreman of his own crew, he had a professional interest. "What's this about a ladder? Can I see too?"

James cracked up, rocking as Liam covered his face with one palm.

Everyone laughed along. Devon and Neil exchanged puzzled glances before Devon shrugged.

"What kind of bullshit is going on now?" Neil smiled good-naturedly.

"Liam's apparently got some ladder piercings, you know...on his peen." James waved toward his crotch. "And I'm guessing by the way Ace and Ruby are practically drooling, that it feels real good when he puts them to use. So maybe you should consider looking into it."

The mischievous twinkle in James's eyes gave away that he was only teasing, but Neil played along. "Nope. No way. I love you, but no one is shoving a needle through my dick repeatedly. If you're into that, you'll have to talk Dave and Kayla into it. That's why you have eight other lovers."

"Oh, right." James looked like he might actually take his husband up on that offer.

"Damn, I already knew you were far more badass than me, but that cinched it." Neil rearranged his package as if just thinking about it pained him. "James, get your shit and let's go. We need your help to get caught up on the house progress at the Powertools site given the late nights we've been putting in on our paid jobs lately."

Their expanded construction business was thriving. It seemed like half of Middletown was trying to hire them for something or other. But Liam got a funny feeling there was some other group activity Neil had in mind for his husband.

Devon grinned. "Yeah. Plus, now I'm worried the Shields are going to corrupt you."

Jordan clutched his chest and rocked while howling at that.

Liam, Ace, and Ruby laughed as they exchanged knowing grins. He should have kept his thoughts to himself, but caught in the warmth of their affectionate gazes, he said, "As if. I've only ever considered having two lovers at once, not eight."

JRad leaned forward, his elbows on his knees. "About fucking time."

James whooped. "First Wren is pregnant, then you three finally hook up, plus Liam's dick is full of sexy jewelry. Is it any wonder I love working here?"

"You're pregnant?" Devon asked, then rushed to hug Wren while Neil shook Jordan and Kason's hands.

"So since it looks like we have a minute..." James leaned in as if he could see through Liam's jeans with the X-ray vision he'd probably pretended to have when aspiring to be a superhero as a kid. "Can I see it?"

"No way." Liam put his hands over his crotch.

"I mean, I'd take a look. For professional research, of course." Blakely glanced over her shoulder slyly.

"It looks better when it's hard." Liam could have kicked himself the instant the words left his mouth.

"I can help you with that," Ace muttered, which got Liam halfway there. "I dare you to show them."

Ruby shifted restlessly and didn't join in the ribbing.

"Do it for science!" James pleaded.

Liam couldn't have said what made him do it, but he side-eyed Ruby. "Should I?"

"Absolutely not." She clamped her hand over his wrist, both thrilling and terrifying him with her possessiveness.

"So it's like that." James pouted, but only a little. "I'm happy for you three. Really."

He hopped up and laid a loud smack on each of their three cheeks. Had he only been goading them for information the whole time?

"I'm glad you're together," JRad said quietly. "I wish you as much happiness as I've found with Lily."

"Wait, I didn't say that. Did I?" Liam stood up, putting a tiny bit of distance between him and Ruby and Ace before he did something stupid and professed his love when they hadn't so much as discussed what they wanted for the future.

He wished he could be as confident as Ace and Ruby. Hell, they were already acting like lovebirds, fawning over each other and touching every chance they could get. They'd twisted so tight around each other the night before, all he could do was watch with envy from his side of the bed.

But apparently that wasn't the right thing to say. Ace locked up tight and Ruby glared at Liam as she kneaded Ace's chest.

"I'm with Ruby," Ace said plainly. He held out his hand to her and she clasped it in her own.

She didn't stop there, though. She knelt over him and kissed him while the rest of the Shields cheered them on. Liam had no idea if they were making out to tease him for being too cowardly to embrace his emotions, to flaunt what he was missing out on, or simply because they fucking loved doing it.

In every scenario, he was screwed.

14

Liam kicked back in a plush leather boardroom chair while JRad took his shift manning the computers in the command station. Ruby had gone on break, whisked away by Sola and Kennedy for a couple hours of girl time. He'd tried to follow but they'd shooed him away, insisting Aarav would be there for backup guard duty. Liam wasn't an idiot. He knew that meant the women were digging for dirt on whatever the fuck was happening between him, Ace, and Ruby.

Maybe after they figured it out they could tell him what the hell he was supposed to do with two amazing people who, for some reason, put up with his shit even when he couldn't pull his head out of his ass long enough to man up and confess he was afraid he'd fucking die without them.

The past couple of days of near constant orgasms had diverted attention from the harder questions they were going to have to figure out answers to soon, but for the moment he was more content than he'd ever thought possible.

JRad didn't turn his chair, continuing to monitor lines of code flying past. The bank ransom deadline loomed, and the masked hacker was going to have to make their move soon. He didn't move, but he cleared his throat.

Ah shit. Here it came. Liam had been waiting for them to be alone.

"Go ahead. Say whatever it is you've been choking down." Liam huffed out a laugh. "You've been right every other time so far. What am I screwing up now?"

"Ace and Ruby look pretty damn happy." JRad hummed. "At least with each other. Have you told them you're crazy about them yet?"

"Probably not the best idea with this case ongoing." Liam folded his arms over his abs and the acid that still churned in his guts at the thought of doing anything that might negatively impact Ace and his concentration in the field. "I think we should save the heavy discussions until after this is wrapped."

"In our line of work, you should never hold back saying something important in case you never get the chance." JRad shook his head.

"Your wife doesn't work with you in the field, does she?" Liam wondered.

"Not regularly, but we met on a case. And it was..." JRad whistled.

"Ruby told me something about a sex drug and some wild shit going down." Liam cocked his head. "Was *that* the case?"

"Yup. Same one where Lucas lost his leg and met the love of his life, who'd been imprisoned and brutalized." JRad scrubbed his hands over his face. "The things we survived together changed us, forever, both for better and for worse. But at the end of the day we're stronger for having gone through it together. You need to trust that they can handle it."

"I don't doubt that for a second." Liam sat up. Was that what Ace and Ruby thought too? That he didn't have faith in them to endure? "It's me I'm worried about. I would lose it entirely if something happened to them, especially because of me. Ace in the field or Ruby because she's associated with us or..."

"What?" JRad asked, this time spinning his chair to meet Liam's gaze.

"What if I'm the top and something happens to me? Don't you worry about that?" Liam winced.

"Of course. That's both your nature and your responsibility. Mine too." JRad waved his hands around him. "But do you think for one second that if the worst came to pass that the rest of the Shields—or, hell, even me—wouldn't look after them for you and make sure no one took advantage of their grief or their submissive tendencies until someone who deserved them came along?"

"Oh." Liam blinked.

"Right." JRad turned back to his work as voices neared, ending their private conversation. Ace ambled through the door talking excitedly with Lucas.

"How was the range?" Liam asked, eager to mull over the ideas JRad had planted in his mind. With a safety net like that, maybe it was possible to finally go after what he'd desperately wished for and yet thought impossible for so long.

"Fucking great." Ace flashed one of the grins that had been achingly sparse lately. "It's only been a few days and I'm hardly missing with my other hand at fifty feet."

"Nice." Liam beamed at him. "I'm proud of you, Ace."

Ace froze and whipped his gaze from Lucas to Liam. "Yeah?"

The reflection of JRad's smile in the monitor made Liam certain he was heading in the right direction. He stood and crossed to his partner, bumping his shoulder into Ace's good side. "Of course. You're doing everything you can to be ready for action."

"I'm *always* ready for action." Ace raised his brows and smirked, which made Lucas snort.

"Good thing," JRad interrupted. "Because here we go. The drive was just activated."

Monitors flashed and things began flying around the screen.

"Go get Ruby!" JRad shouted. "I need her. Now."

"Can't we just text her? It'll be faster." Ace had his phone out of his pocket.

"Tried that. She's not answering. Find her." JRad didn't pause whatever he was doing, but there was an edge to his tone that Liam didn't care for.

He exchanged a worried glance with Ace before they bolted for the elevator and hit the button ten thousand times in a row. "Fuck this. Stairs."

They turned together and slammed the stairwell door open before taking the stairs three at a time up to the fourth floor. They charged down the hall and nearly smashed through the door. Scanning the apartment, there was no sign of the women.

Aarav stood there, gun drawn, pointed directly at their faces. Now Liam knew how Cash had felt knowing the sniper had them in his sights and didn't miss. Ever.

"What the fuck is wrong with you two? Do you have a death wish?" Aarav put his gun back in his holster.

Until there was a shriek from the direction of the bathroom. Liam bellowed, "Ruby!"

Then he sprinted for the bathroom. This time he did kick in the door. The frame splintered and the doorknob stuck, pinning it open as he propelled it into the drywall. All he could see was red.

Everywhere.

Splatters on the floor, the sink, the shower, and all over Ruby's porcelain skin.

Jesus fucking Christ.

His heart shattered and hope vanished. Whatever foolish thoughts he'd been having downstairs evaporated as every nightmare he'd had came true before his eyes. He'd taken responsibility for Ruby and Ace, and yet he'd failed them both. He had never deserved them, couldn't protect them, and now he'd regret it for the rest of his life.

Ruby gawked at the door as Liam charged through it as if he was racing into hell to face the devil himself. She'd never been afraid of him, not because of his size or his need for control, but in that moment, she realized how terrifying it would be to be his enemy.

"What in the hell is wrong with you?" Ruby gasped as Sola instinctively stepped in front of her, brandishing a razor as an impromptu weapon.

Damn. Living with a bunch of assassins had its moments.

Kennedy put her hands up and started talking in her soothing doctor voice. "Calm down, Liam. It's fine. It's just dye. We were helping Ruby with her hair and the bottle exploded."

Ruby looked down at herself and the mess and realized what had happened. He'd thought...

Oh shit.

"Yeah, totally fine. So sorry about your bathroom, though. I'm not sure this white stone or the grout will ever be the same." Ruby offered a wan smile.

Then she nearly had a heart attack when Liam's knees buckled. He sank to the floor and braced his hands on the sloppy tiles, his back heaving. Kennedy rushed to his side and so did Ace. "Breathe, buddy. You're fine. It's okay. Everything's good. Ruby is safe."

Stunned, Ruby started toweling herself off. She'd buy him a new one to replace the definitely ruined terrycloth. But before she could kiss the shit out of him for caring so much, she was stopped in her tracks by Ace. He looked up and met her stare. "JRad needs you. The drive. It's on."

"Fuck nuggets!" She grabbed her phone and saw she had seventeen missed texts. She put her hand on Liam's shoulder and squeezed before running out the door, Sola and Aarav right on her ass. "Sorry, Liam. Sorry!"

The whole ride down to the command center, all she could think of was the damage she'd unintentionally done. She groaned, feeling queasy. "Did you see the look on his face?"

"Not one I'd like to remember." Sola rubbed her temple. "That's gonna sting for a while."

Aarav tried to help. "It's not easy, what we do, and especially not when our loved ones are involved. He'll come around."

"I don't know about that." Ruby kept replaying Liam crashing to the bathroom floor over and over until the elevator doors opened and she had to concentrate on other things.

"What the fuck happened to you?" Lucas stared as she burst into the command center and flew to her seat.

JRad did a double take when he looked at her too. "You okay?"

"Unfortunate hair dye accident. Liam, though, he might not make it." She clicked on the files JRad had already queued up for her and got to work. "He thought someone had offed me."

"Oh fuck." JRad groaned. "He was coming around, too."

"You think?" Ruby wished she could sort it out, but the case required her undivided attention. She stripped as much information as she could as quickly as she could. Who knew how long it would be before the masked hacker realized she was tracking his every move?

"It's here." Ruby highlighted a section of code and flung it back to JRad. "That's their location. You work on that and I'll make sure the rest of my security measures are holding. I only need a few more bits to come up with a quarantine protocol we can sell to the banks and publish so we can disarm this shit for good."

Jordan and James must have joined them, though she didn't turn around to verify. James handed her a headset and Jordan spoke into her ear. Well, into the whole team's ears, she suspected. "Aven is standing by. Let me know if we need the chopper or a plane based on distance."

Ruby focused on the ones and zeros and commands zooming through her mind. Talking to herself, but also for JRad's benefit, she said, "Confirm security measures holding. No copies have been made except the one I just exported for our use. We have everything we need, including a decrypted list of contacts for sales and blackmailing and the identities of the original coders. If you can destroy that drive, and the only physical proof of this shit with it, I can do the rest from here. We've got this."

"Good work, Ruby." Jordan's praise warmed her, though not as much as a hug from Liam would have right then.

Focus. She worked furiously, securing everything they needed and developing her antidote code so she barely registered it when JRad barked, "Chopper. The signal is originating about 185 miles from here. Coordinates on screen."

"Team of six," Jordan snapped. "Liam, Ace, Tavish, and Legend, you have unfinished business with this asshole. Aarav cover their asses. Kennedy, you're in. Stay with Aven in the chopper unless needed."

Ruby ignored the implications. If they had a use for Kennedy, it was a bad day.

"Be safe, babe," Marcus murmured before he and Knox took turns kissing Kennedy.

They hated letting her go without them, but they did. They trusted her. And Ruby would have to do the same for Liam and Ace, though she'd be lying if she said she didn't feel some kind of way differently than she had when they'd left on missions in the past.

Jordan interrupted their sweet goodbye with a chilling realization. "Given the information Ruby has now—which will allow us to shut down the entire operation—and the confirmation that the data has not been replicated, there's no need to take our masked man alive anymore. Do so if possible. If not...it's more important to destroy that drive."

"Will do," Ace promised.

Liam was silent.

"Guys, can I talk to you?" Ruby asked.

Ace rushed to her side but not Liam.

"We shouldn't distract you right now," he said quietly, though Jordan didn't object.

"Fuck that." Ruby reached up with one hand and dragged Ace to her for a scorching kiss. "Pass that along to Liam for me, would you? And come home safe. I love you, both of you."

"I love you too, Ruby." Ace smiled, his forehead resting against hers for a long moment before he separated them. Elation bubbled through her veins like champagne until she realized that Liam hadn't said it back, nor had he taken a single step closer to them.

She and Ace turned together toward him. He stared, stony faced, red dye smeared over his palms. He looked down at the stains and then at them, then at the thick red liquid again before pivoting on his booted heel and departing.

Beside her, JRad cursed.

"Aven is landing on the roof in two minutes. Get your asses up there." James winced as he looked to Ace and Ruby and mouthed *sorry*.

Ace bolted after Liam and the rest of the field team.

And then they were gone, the command center eerily quiet, and Ruby had to concentrate on the job at hand. But all she could see burned into her mind was Liam and the look on his face when he'd thought she'd been grievously injured.

Maybe no matter how much he wanted to, he couldn't open himself up to that kind of agony. Could she really blame him? He'd been honest about it from the start.

If she'd fallen for him anyway, it was her own fault, not his.

15

———

The overwhelming scent of pine, dirt, and night air assaulted Ace's senses as he loped through the woods. Those hours running on the Shields' track were paying off now. Aven had set the chopper down out of sight and hearing from the coordinates JRad had fed her.

Dodging tree trunks and leaping fallen branches, Liam raced beside him. Legend and Tavish, in proper tactical gear instead of his usual kilt, mirrored them a bit farther south while Aarav took a different path along the river that cut a chasm in the cliff top they were rushing along.

Ace's heart pounded but not from exertion. More from anxiety.

Would he be able to do his part for the team? And if they made it out alive, could he convince Liam that Ruby was their future?

Ace shook his head and fixated on putting one boot in front of the other, making as little sound as possible as he dashed through the forest. This wasn't the time to worry about that shit.

Aarav came over their comms. "I'm in place. I have the crack JRad told us about from the satellite image lined up in my sights. I would say you're wrong and that there's no way that's the entrance to some computer freak's hideout, but I just spotted two guards on patrol. Let me know when you're about to start your rappel and I will get rid of them for you."

It would have to be some top-secret lair, wouldn't it? What was with bad guys and these ridiculous outposts? They watched too damn many movies.

The team was going to be an easy target as they descended to what was essentially the back door of the place, since they had no hope of crashing through the reinforced steel doors at the main entrance. Oh well, it was a nice evening for an excursion at least. His night vision goggles made the twinkling stars overhead brighter than the lights on Main Street back in Middletown.

Under different circumstances, Ace would love to be camped out under them with Liam and Ruby.

"We're close," Liam told Aarav.

"Us too," Legend said. "I can see the edge."

The four of them made quick work of setting and checking their gear before hovering on the cusp of the precipice. Ace looked up and caught Liam's golden stare fixed on him. "Ready. Are you?"

Ace hesitated the briefest of moments before he nodded. "Let's get this done."

And what would come after?

No time to discuss now.

Aarav's voice was flat and emotionless, though his affair with Sola and Cash had made it apparent that only applied when he was doing his job. Like now. "Two fewer problems to worry about. You're clear."

Liam tossed a hand signal to Ace, Legend, and Tavish. The four of them went over at once, harder for someone to stop them that way rather than picking them off one by one if they went single file. Cool air rushed against Ace's face and gravity tugged at him in his harness as he kicked off the stone, lowering himself several feet at a time.

It didn't take long before they'd landed on a dusty ledge, dropped their equipment, and crept to the back door.

"I'm in on their surveillance." Ruby's voice was a welcome friend over the comms. "Inside the door, two guys are shooting the shit. You should be able to catch them off guard. Beyond that, things get a little hazy—that's a lot of rock for a signal to penetrate—but it looks like you need to head north east down the passage."

JRad added, "Heat signature data makes me think there are at least three people in the room with the drive and four more manning the gates. Hopefully they'll be smart enough to bail when they realize what's going on down below."

Jordan jumped in. "Legend, Tavish, you two take the pair by the door. Once that's dealt with, push forward to the front to keep those four from coming up behind Liam and Ace. You two are on the drive."

He didn't say it, but it was apparent he also meant they were likely going to have to deal with the masked man who'd threatened Ruby. Ace was more than happy to handle that task.

Ruby again. "I've almost got the door open. Ready?"

Liam confirmed, "Yes."

"Okay...Go." A metal click accompanied her order.

Ace and Liam covered Tavish and Legend as they stormed the entrance. As Ruby had promised, the two men there were caught flat footed, expecting their buddies who'd gone to check the perimeter instead of four highly trained assassins.

Legend and Tavish each dropped one, then stood to the side, allowing Liam and Ace to rush past in the stone corridor. They took the fork toward the direction Ruby had indicated and slowed down as Tavish and Legend departed in the opposite direction.

On their own, Liam took the lead.

Ace checked behind them as they made their way deeper into the hacker's den toward the blue glow that painted the stone walls. Good thing he wasn't claustrophobic because thinking of the weight of the entire mountain pressing in on them wasn't very comfortable.

From ahead, he heard voices. Liam must have too because he slowed, inching toward an opening on the left. It didn't take more than a sentence or two for Ace to recognize the voice.

He'd heard it that night all this had started and again when the masked man had laid his hands on Ruby. Now that it wasn't distorted, he noticed something he hadn't previously. An accent. German, he thought.

"You getting that?" Jordan asked as he too must have heard the same. The gear they were wearing was a hell of a lot better than some shitty security camera.

"Yeah, boss." Ruby confirmed.

"Someone, go get me—" Jordan cut his comms, probably to keep from distracting the fields agents from a sidebar conversation in the command center. What angle was he working and would it help them nail this bastard who'd threatened Ruby?

A stifled snarl bared Ace's teeth.

Liam waved his hand parallel to the ground in a signal for *calm down.*

Not likely.

Then he gestured between them and pointed to the opening. They were going in.

Ace nodded.

Liam stared straight into his eyes as if saying a million things Ace couldn't hear but felt soul deep and held up three fingers.

James came over the comms. "Ace and Liam are going in. In three...two..."

Then they were charging. When they burst into the room, they faced three men. Two seated closer to the entrance and the masked man sneering at them from the head of the room filled with electronics and blinking lights. Ace took the guy on the left and Liam the one on the right. He nailed the guy in the temple with the butt of his gun, knocking him to the floor, unconscious.

Liam's charge tumbled to the ground nearby.

And then they were there, face to face with the bastard who'd tormented Ruby for the sake of some cash. Okay, a hell of a lot of it. But still.

Ace had never been so angry on a job before and he recognized that it probably wasn't smart. But none of that fucking mattered when the asshole who'd hidden behind that stupid mask raised his hand, and in it was a gun. He pointed it straight at Liam's heart.

Whether he knew how to use it or not, Ace wasn't about to hang around to find out.

"I remember you. Going to try harder this time?" The jerk cackled, his expensive watch flashing in the twinkling lights of the computers. "We all know how this is going to end since you clearly need me alive to figure out my code."

"That's where you're wrong, asshole." Ace charged him, crashing into his outstretched arm. "Ruby had you beat before you even knew it."

The two of them rolled, preventing Liam from getting a clean shot. But at least that gun wasn't aimed at him anymore. Ace took an unlucky tumble, hitting his head on an outcropping of rock. The impact made him see stars and lose his grip on his weapon, which skittered to the side, out of reach.

The hacker took his chance. He swung his elbow and hit Ace directly in his bad arm. Ace howled, rolling on the floor in agony while Liam roared as if he'd been the one wounded.

But Ace ignored the pain radiating from his wound and climbed to his feet while subduing the hacker as best he could without using one entire side of his body. Liam still couldn't get a shot off with Ace in the way and there wasn't time or room to maneuver. So Ace held out his uninjured hand and smiled at Liam, who immediately understood.

Without an instant of hesitation, Liam tossed his gun to Ace, who caught it in the hand he'd been practicing with at the range. He swung around, aimed, and fired point blank. The hacker would never bother Ruby again.

"Guys!" Ruby shouted. "Two more incoming. Legend and Tavish cleared the rest."

Ace looked to Liam, who shook his head. "You've got this."

Liam threw himself flat on the ground to keep out of

Ace's way as a flurry of boot steps clomped near. The evil fucks didn't make it two feet over the threshold before Ace nailed them both between the eyes and they piled up on top of the rest before they could so much as glance in Liam's direction, never mind threaten him.

Liam rolled to his back on the ground and looked up at Ace in awe. "You're amazing."

"Nice work, everyone." Jordan came over the comms. "Get that drive and get the fuck out."

"You need me to peel that mask off so you can get some pictures of the perp?" Ace didn't relish the thought but he'd do it if he had to.

"Nah, I already know who it is." Jordan cursed. "Albert Suisse. Cash confirmed his voice, and that watch was his prized possession. A ridiculously overpriced one-of-a-kind made exclusively for him."

"Seriously?" Liam gawked. "Why?"

"I guess we know how he was so successful so young. It's a special sort of cheating to gain enough power to make your own rules." Jordan sounded disgusted. "Well, not this time. He won't be getting rich off ruining the lives of my team. Fuck that. Aarav, circle around front and make sure no one else tries to squat in the place. Nolan, Marcus, Knox, Sola, Ransom, and Levi will be there in forty-five minutes to document the scene, verify identities, and dispose of the bodies, then clean out the rest of the equipment. I'll take care of coming up with a cover story. By morning, it will be like that hellhole never existed."

Ace went to the computer rack and unplugged the lone drive set up in the center like a shrine.

"That's the one," Ruby confirmed. "Bring it to me so I can decommission it permanently and we'll be set."

"It's over." James sighed for them all.

Ace crossed to Liam, who was sitting up, and held out his good hand to help him to his feet. Liam didn't stop there, he continued his forward momentum to crush Ace in a bear hug that practically lifted him off his feet.

Then Liam kissed the shit out of him. "Ace, that was the hottest thing I've ever seen in my life."

"Hey, I thought me tied to your bed had that honor," Ruby added, making them aware that everyone back at headquarters could hear and see through their body cams.

Oh well. It was finally his turn for payback after the endless sickeningly sweet and sexy shit he'd walked in on this past year.

"It will be, when we get home." Liam retrieved Ace's gun and gave it back to him, exchanging it for his own.

Ace clicked off his comms and put his hand over his body cam in case Liam was about to let Ruby down again. He motioned for Liam to do the same then asked, "You really mean that?"

"Yeah. It's about time I accept that for some reason, the two of you picked me even though you're plenty capable of taking care of yourselves."

"I'm not broken anymore."

"You never were, Ace. I was." Liam kissed him again. "But you...and Ruby...you fixed me. I love you. Both of you."

Ace reengaged his equipment.

"Aven, how fast can you get us home?" he shouted. He took Liam's hand and dragged him toward the exit, willing to sprint the entire way to the chopper if it got them there one moment sooner. Because he had plans for the rest of his night.

And the rest of his life.

16

L iam swallowed hard and paused with his fingers around the door handle to the Shields' headquarters.

"If you can charge into a cave full of criminals who want to kill you, you can talk about your feelings with one adorable, extra-redheaded woman," Ace teased.

"I'd much rather go fight some more bad guys." Liam yanked the door open. "At least I don't have to worry about fucking them up. I mean, that's kind of the point."

"You're going to do fine. Be honest and trust that she can handle herself. Same as I can." Ace shoved Liam toward the command center and the woman who would almost certainly be waiting within. The impact wasn't insubstantial.

"Glad to see your arm is doing okay," Liam groused.

"You heard Kennedy." Ace repeated himself for the four-thousandth time, as if neither of them could believe how lucky he'd been. "The impact only seems to have bruised the flesh against the internal hardware. I'll go for the follow up scans and shit she wants tomorrow. But it doesn't hurt near as bad as it has in the past. It's good enough for tonight."

Liam sighed his relief at that. But it was short-lived because the instant he saw Ruby still hammering away at her supercomputer he tensed again.

"Welcome home," she said, without turning to face them. "One second, I almost have this fully executed. Just confirming. Yes, the blockchain is restored to its original state. The digital wallet balances, including my own, are correct, and I've released the preventative anti-virus protocols to every financial institution that funded Jordan's infosec operation. They approved the full bonus to keep Albert's involvement as hushed as the rest."

"Great work, kid." JRad held out his fist and Ruby bumped it, a massive grin illuminating her features.

"I couldn't have done it without you."

"Yeah, you could have, but I'm glad I was able to help." JRad looked from her to Liam and Ace. His meaning wasn't lost on any of them. Without his advice, they might never have taken their relationship beyond the friend zone.

"Jordan, can I talk to these two in private?" Liam asked their boss since they hadn't yet held a proper debrief.

"Only if by *talk,* you mean *fuck,*" Ruby mumbled under her breath, reminding him of the day she'd blasted through his initial resistance. From next to her, James snorted.

"Yeah. Go ahead." Jordan appraised them before saying, "I think everything urgent is wrapped for now. Let's reconvene at eight tomorrow morning when the cleanup crew is back too."

"Thanks, boss." Ruby sighed and stretched as she rose. Her face was pale and there were circles under her eyes he'd never seen before this week. Was he really good for her?

"You look so tired." Liam brushed his thumb over her cheek. "We don't have to do this now."

"Yes, we do," both Ruby and Ace said in unison. They each took one of Liam's hands and dragged him through the lobby.

This time Liam didn't hesitate. Before the doors of the elevator had fully slid shut, he pressed Ruby up against the wall of the car and kissed her until the world spun around them.

From the hallway, Tavish and Legend's whistles and catcalls cheered them on. Ruby put one hand out, fishing for Ace, who came near and nudged Liam aside. He took Liam's place, kissing Ruby with every bit as much passion if slightly less desperation.

Liam led the way to their apartment. He was hoping it might be Ruby's home now too, if he hadn't fucked up one time too many. Once inside he didn't pause in the living room but instead took them straight to his bedroom, where he intended to keep them as often as possible.

He flicked on his bedside lamp then he turned to face them. "I'm sorry I freaked out before we left, Ruby. It was a shock and everything that keeps me up at night and—"

"I get it. I do." She hugged him tight. "You see firsthand how horribly things can go in life sometimes. I didn't mean to scare you like that. But if I can tolerate you and Ace going out in the field, you're going to have to figure out how to deal with the fact that life is never certain so we can at least make the most of whatever time we have together."

"I always said she was way smarter than us." Ace beamed at her.

"You're right. I know you are. But you might have to remind me often that we're here and alive and together." Liam scrunched his eyes shut. "It's me who has the issue. Not you two. On the flight back I asked Kennedy to schedule me some time with the team therapist. I want to work on this so it doesn't impact you two anymore. You're capable and so strong and...incredible."

"Did you see how Ace nailed those dirtbags earlier?" Ruby stared at him with adoration.

"I did. Had a front-row seat." Liam nodded. "It was magnificent."

Ruby turned to Ace and petted his chest. "It turned me on to see you so sure of yourself again. I'm probably not supposed to admit that, but...there you go."

"Fortunately, I have no doubt I can fix that condition for you." Ace stole another kiss from her, this one longer and more languid than the peck he'd given her in the elevator.

Liam cleared his throat. "There's one more thing I want to say before we lose our clothes and I forget how to form full sentences."

"Yeah?" Ruby raised a brow, daring him to ruin the moment.

"I love you. Both of you." He stared at the ceiling then said in a rush. "I have for a long time. I'm sorry I didn't tell you sooner, but I was scared shitless."

"I know." Ace grinned, then let him off the hook. "Congrats on finally finding your balls."

Ruby snorted and smacked Ace playfully. "I bet you knew where those were all along."

"They're about to be on your tongue." Liam growled and stalked closer to them. "Are you sure you want to rile me right before I'm in charge of passing out orgasms around here?"

"Uh huh. Yup. I definitely do." Ace's flippant reply signaled the return of his spontaneous and sometimes rash nature. It drove Liam nuts, but he also admired how free Ace was and he never wanted to be the cause of snuffing out that side of him again.

Liam growled and charged Ace, hooking one arm in his crotch and the other over his shoulder. He tossed Ace onto the bed and tumbled after him, being careful but not overly so. Hell, he was partially made of titanium, not glass. Ruby bounced beside them as she joined the fray.

While she and Ace alternated laughing, wrestling, and making out, Liam got to work. He stripped Ace's tactical pants off with a single yank that resulted in a few torn seams. Too bad.

And soon all three of them were naked.

Whatever had happened in the field, or maybe their mutual understanding about their relationship status going forward, had lit something in Ace. He didn't waste any time rolling Ruby to her back and covering her, their bodies pressed together from shoulders to toes.

Liam reached between his legs and cupped Ace's balls as he feasted on Ruby's mouth and they fed each other a series of moans. Kneeling beside them, Liam took his cock in his hand and began to stroke. He'd never get tired of watching them please each other for their own benefit in addition to his.

When Ace began to slither down Ruby's torso, licking his lips as if intent on devouring her, she stopped him by cupping his elbow. "I'm plenty ready and I don't want to wait. Get inside me, Ace."

Liam groaned.

Ace encircled the base of his cock and wedged his knees between Ruby's. Liam helped by taking hold of her thigh and yanking it wide to make room for his partner. She gasped and arched on the bed, welcoming Ace into her open arms and into her body.

He flew to her, fitting the glistening head of his cock to her entrance while Liam stroked the hair back from her face and studied her expression. If they went too fast, and spooked her even a little, he'd know and slow Ace down.

In the meantime, Liam dipped his thumb into her mouth and muttered a curse when she sucked, swirling her tongue around it and even nipping him kind of hard. Fuck.

Ace did one better.

The moment he'd penetrated the tight ring of muscles at Ruby's entrance and his head slipped deeper into her core, he turned his face and took Liam's cock into his mouth. Ace had always gotten off on a good blow job, but apparently sucking and fucking together was even better. He groaned around Liam's shaft, sending vibrations straight to Liam's balls, and took him a little too deep, too fast.

When he choked, and thrust hard and fast into Ruby, Liam rubbed his back, soothing him even as he tried to calm him. "Easy, Ace. I'm not going anywhere. Neither is Ruby. You can have as much of us as you want."

"Yeah. What he said." Ruby wrapped her legs around his hips and rocked upward to meet his next—more measured—thrust. "You can do this for as long and as often as you want. Damn."

Her head thrashed on the pillow as her body accommodated Ace's invasion. Liam would never say so, but he was jealous as fuck. His cock couldn't wait for its turn to be buried in her steamy pussy. "Don't worry, Ruby. We can probably keep this up all night if we take turns."

Her gaze flew to his. "I was kind of hoping you wouldn't."

"Huh?" Ace paused and tipped his head. "Do you want me to stop?"

"Fuck no." Ruby hugged him to her. "I don't want one of you at a time. I want you both together. You promised."

Liam stiffened. "We should work up to that."

"I'm telling you that's what I want and that I can handle it. And if it turns out I'm wrong, I swear I will say so." Ruby clutched his thigh. "I need to be between you, Liam. Please?"

There was no way he could resist her begging as she looked up at him with wide eyes and a mouth glossy and plump from their kisses.

Ace looked up at him, waiting for direction.

"Flip onto your back, Ace." Liam took over jerking off as Ace's mouth moved farther away. And soon, Ace was settled with Ruby draped over him, his cock still firmly embedded in her.

"Fuck yes, I love being on the bottom." Ace moaned. "Feeling both of you pressing down on me, blanketing me. I hope you know I can't last like this for long."

"Some really smart people told me something doesn't have to last forever to be worth it." Liam planted his hand between Ruby's shoulder blades and mashed her to Ace as he balanced on one knee between their tangled legs. His other foot he put flat on the bed near their hips, giving himself as much room to maneuver, leverage, and the best angle possible to work himself into Ruby alongside Ace.

His balls drew up tight to his torso at the thought of being bound together with them, both him and Ace held tight together by Ruby. It was everything he'd wished for but had been too afraid to believe could be possible.

Liam tapped his cock on Ace's balls, making his partner curse and jerk. Ruby clung tight, riding him as Liam's dick traced the prominent vein on the underside of Ace's shaft straight to her pussy. He smacked her ass a few times before wedging himself beside Ace at her entrance.

"Let me in, Ruby," he coached as he rubbed the sting from her cheeks.

And when she relaxed beneath his palm, Liam advanced. The pressure built until he almost retreated, but she hooked her arm around behind her and dug her fingers into his ass to drag him closer. Liam bit her shoulder and his hips twitched involuntarily, burying him the barest bit inside her.

All three of them moaned.

Liam's breathing was ragged as he fucked into her, caressing Ace's shaft with both his own flesh and his piercings as he tucked himself into Ruby.

"Son of a bitch." Ace pounded the mattress. "That feels so fucking good."

It did to Liam too. The way the metal tugged on his dick as he brushed against Ace only added to the heat of Ruby's pussy searing him and the impossible tightness of the grip she had on them.

"How is Ruby?" Liam asked Ace.

Ace stared up into her eyes, smiling as he brushed the hair from her face and kissed her with thousands of butterfly kisses. "She's amazing."

"She is." Liam caressed her back and dipped his thumb between her cheeks to press against her tight ass. Maybe soon she'd want to explore there too.

Ruby cried out. "Keep going. Don't stop."

Liam obliged, first moving forward until he bottomed out within her before retreating. He fucked slowly and deliberately at first before speeding up once he was sure all three of them could handle it. At least for a little while. Something that intense wouldn't linger.

"Am I crushing you, Ace?" Liam asked when his partner seemed like he was gasping and panting.

"No. Just trying not to come."

"Already?" Liam grinned. "You're going to wait for Ruby."

"Not long." She squirmed between them, setting them both off.

"But someday, maybe we can flip." Ace opened his eyes then and speared Liam with a gaze so full of sexual intent that Liam's balls clenched.

"You want to fuck me?" Liam asked.

"Would you let me?" Ace wondered.

And though he could honestly say he'd never considered it before, Liam didn't hesitate. "Fuck yeah."

Ruby shuddered between them, her pussy wringing them as the first feathering clenches of her orgasm began. As if that alone meant something to Ace, he hugged Ruby with one arm and Liam with the other. He pulled them to him as if he never intended to let go.

Liam knew what they needed and he gave it to them, fucking into Ruby with a flurry of fast, short jabs that rubbed her clit against Ace's torso in a rhythm that was impossible for any of them to resist.

Ruby tossed her head and shattered. She didn't need to tell them she was coming when the primal sounds she made echoed the pulsing of her body around them. Her orgasm lured Liam and Ace into their own. Their cocks erupted at the same instant, painting Ruby's pussy and each other's cocks with the proof of how intensely they could affect each other.

They overflowed her stretched pussy with their releases and kept pumping into her with repetitive bursts for what seemed like minutes. Liam had never experienced pleasure that complete or satisfying. And when, finally, he softened enough that he slipped from Ruby's body along with Ace, he wobbled to the bathroom on trembling legs to prepare warm, wet washcloths so he could care for them properly.

It brought him nearly as much gratification as his colossal orgasm to tend to them as they often did to him. But this time, when he finished and ultimately rejoined them in bed, he didn't creep around to the far edge. Instead, he crawled onto the bed from its foot and went straight up the center.

He fit himself between Ace and Ruby on his back then drew both of them to him. They draped themselves over his thighs and chest while kissing each other sweetly when they met in the middle. Only after they'd spent eons exploring this newfound familiarity did Liam dip his head and seal his mouth to theirs.

He'd never experienced that sort of unhurried, lingering affection with the bone-deep knowledge that they had more than one night to spend exploring each other and what they became when the three of them were joined completely, not only physically to the depth of their souls.

But he discovered he liked it a hell of a lot.

Liam squeezed each of them with one of his arms until Ruby squeaked and Ace huffed out a laugh. "I love you too, Liam. And you, Ruby."

Ruby beamed at them, a single tear slipping from the corner of her eye.

Liam kissed it away and said, "He's right, you know. I love you both. Thank you for giving me one more chance. I swear to you both I will not fuck it up."

Ruby nuzzled her face into his beard and entwined her fingers with Ace's. "I love both of you big, dumb idiots so much."

Liam barked out a laugh and Ace grinned at her. They teamed up and tickled her until things got a little out of hand, and Ace redeemed Liam's backdoor rain check while they took turns eating Ruby out. It was hours before they crashed, exhausted into a deep and peaceful sleep in each other's arms.

They proved to Liam over and over that his life could be far more wondrous than he'd ever hoped if only they relied on each other's strengths rather than worrying about their weaknesses. Because the truth was that together, when they balanced each other out, they didn't have many of those.

17

Karolena's gaze darted around the lobby of the Shields Security Services lobby as she waited for the office manager to collect her for her interview. When she'd spoken to him on the phone he'd seemed friendly and easy going, chipper, and entirely non-threatening. However as she sat, crossing and recrossing her legs, back straight, trying not to fidget with the hem of the black skirt she'd picked up from a thrift store nearby, a gaggle of colossal men and intense women crisscrossed the space.

Maybe this had been a horrible idea.

The hairs on her arms stood on end and her survival instincts went on high alert being near so many folks that reminded her of Vladimir's men. Unofficial soldiers. People who made their own rules and enforced them by whatever means necessary. She knew their type too damn well.

Karolena flipped her long platinum hair over her shoulder and clutched the folder keeping her resume wrinkle-free. She needed this job. One she could actually do with her very limited skill set. Plus it came with a place to stay. A very convenient spot to hide.

Besides, there were some differences between the cold mercenaries she'd grown up around and the Shields. Laughter rang down the hallway. People actually looked her in the eye and said hello when they discovered her perched on the chair in the high-traffic area. One man—the one with red hair who wore a kilt of all things, which showed off legs sexier than a man had a right to—had even held the door for her. Not because of how powerful her ex was, but because he had at least some manners. When she'd thanked him, he'd grinned and said you're welcome with an accent that outstripped even his legs.

Karolena should have turned around and left right then.

Especially since the giant, dark-haired guy right behind him had grinned and elbowed the Scottish door-holder as if he had noticed his colleague lingering too long, as she had herself. The very last thing she needed in her life was more complications or love affairs with dangerous men.

Look how that had worked out. Not that she'd exactly had a choice when it came to Vladimir. After her father had essentially traded her to the kingpin in exchange for his own life, it wasn't like she could tell Vladimir to fuck off in the years that had followed.

She swallowed hard, debating bolting. But what options did she have?

Exactly none.

A man with sandy hair and a compact build practically skipped out of an office wearing a neon-yellow polo, matching sneakers, and a pair of extraordinarily well-tailored, if ass-and-bulge-hugging trousers. He was nothing like the rest of them, thank God. "Karolena? I'm James."

He held out his hand to her as she stood and didn't try to win a pissing match or intimidate her with the crush of his fingers when they shook. Her nerves settled some as he ushered her into a quieter space filled with pictures of a group of nine people that most often featured him at their center.

"Have a seat. So sorry to keep you waiting. As you can see, everyone's running around last minute getting ready for the party that's about to start. I probably should have had you come in tomorrow instead of squeezing in your interview at the end of the day, but...I'm not going to lie... I'm kind of desperate to find someone to help us out."

Well, that made two of them. "It's no trouble at all. Thank you for inviting me to speak to you about the position."

James grinned and waved her off. "It's okay to relax. We're not especially formal around here and whoever we bring onboard will pretty much end up as part of our family. Since we all live and work here, and it's literally our job to find stuff out about people...well, our professional boundaries aren't very clear. How does that make you feel?"

Horrified. Karolena schooled her expression, though. If she could smile politely at public functions after being mistreated in private, lying to the man she was determined to turn into her boss was no trouble at all. She would have to be careful to keep them from discovering too much about her past. How hard could that be?

"It's fine." She shrugged. "I tend to keep to myself. So other than making sure this place is spotless—which seems like plenty to occupy me—you won't have to worry about me getting tangled up with anyone."

Karolena got the feeling that her answers were much less important than whatever vibe James was trying to pick up from her as he studied her a little too intently for her own comfort. He surprised her when he asked, "You know this is a shitty job, right? There's a lot of us and we're often distracted by important stuff. The whole reason I'm hiring someone is because they're driving me nuts with how sloppy they are. They don't mean to be gross, but they have other priorities and you're going to have to put up with what I can't stand anymore."

She chuckled at his bluntness. Karolena couldn't accuse him of being dishonest or sugarcoating things, and somehow that made her feel much better. She shrugged one shoulder. "One man's trash is another woman's employment."

When James simply sat and let the silence linger, she filled it in with a hint of her own truth. "You've seen my resume. It's sparse. I never went to college. Don't have any experience. But I want to stand on my own and that means working my way up from the very bottom. If you give me this job, I will do my best to make sure you never trip over another dirty towel in the gym you said is onsite or have to deal with stacks of pizza boxes like that enormous one I spied outside the kitchen doorway."

"They eat so fucking much." James rubbed his temples.

As if on cue, a box van with the logo of the restaurant and pastry shop down the street pulled into the lot outside James's office window. Tables were set up in the grass, draped with cheery cloths and covered by white tents. It looked like children's games were off to one corner and there were enough folding chairs scattered around to accommodate at least fifty people.

"I'm sorry, I'm going to have to cut our talk short." James looked over his shoulder at the chaos unfolding around the picturesque pond out back.

Karolena frowned. She'd hoped to lock this in. "What can I do to convince you I'm the right person for this position?"

"Oh, I'm already sold." James beamed at her as he turned around. "You had me at hard work and low drama. And being unafraid of these assholes and their mess. Besides, you were the only person who applied. The job is yours if you're sure you want it."

Karolena couldn't help it. She grinned right back at him. It had been so long since she'd had reason to do that, the motion felt rusty but she didn't care.

After all, surrounding herself with a gaggle of security goons might be the only way to keep herself safe. For the first time in a long time, Karolena took a deep breath. She stuck out her hand and shook James's once more. "I'll take it.

"Great. When can you start?" James leaned in. "If you want, you're welcome to join us for the party. It's kind of a big night here. We received a commission from a very large job we completed recently and everyone made it through in one piece. There's going to be food, and music by our own resident band, and even fireworks later. Afterward...well...you can just keep staying. Your apartment is emptied of personal belongings but furnished as the position description said, since one of our female agents decided to move in with her boyfriends."

"Boyfriends?" Had she heard wrong?

James's carefully chosen words made it obvious this was one final test. "Yeah. A lot of the people who work here are in non-traditional, poly relationships. Myself included. That's not a problem, is it?"

"Not to me." Karolena wondered what it would be like to have the freedom to love whomever she chose, whether that was one person or several. But she didn't even dare to dream that big. A safe haven and a salary she could use to start building a new life was more than she'd expected.

If she'd been alone in a bathroom right then, she might have wept.

James stood and she mimicked him as they headed for the door. The instant he opened it, the din of people moving around, music from the party site, and the flurry of activity from the catering crew became more apparent. This time it didn't unsettle her as much.

"Welcome onboard." James smiled kindly at her as he handed her a set of keys.

To her own place. He had no idea the gift he'd given her.

Except he took a little of the shine off when he said, "Let me get someone to show you around while I'm busy with the celebration details."

Before she could assure him she'd rather explore on her own, he called out to the door-holder and his giant friend. Okay, so her luck hadn't improved *that* much.

"Hey, Tavish, Legend." James waved them over and they came at a jog. "Come here. I want you to meet your new neighbor."

"What?" Oh no. Not only working for them but living next door? Karolena tried not to let her eyes bug out but they must have noticed.

Tavish chuckled as Legend introduced them and

confirmed that they did indeed live across the hall from the vacant apartment. Her new home.

"If you don't mind, I'll leave you three to it so I can get out there before these dumbasses set something on fire or—"

No sooner had the words left his mouth than a *boom* rattled the windows.

Legend threw an arm protectively around Karolena and Tavish stepped in between her and the plate glass. Even as strangers, their first instinct was to shelter her, not exploit her. But despite their reflexive reactions, there was no attack. No assault.

Instead, a guy with perfect slicked back hair ran away from a crate marked flammable as another dude covered in black-and-gray tattoos wearing an arm brace was tailed by a huge blond guy with a beard. More fireworks shot from the side of the container that had obviously gone off by accident.

They were aimed directly at a hideous green vehicle with a black pipe sticking up from the hood, dark tinted glass, and wheels that were far too big for its tiny frame.

"Not my baby!" James shrieked, and ran outside as Tavish and Legend began cracking up.

"You're laughing at his car getting destroyed?" Karolena flung out her hands as she turned on them. Maybe they weren't so different from the men who'd made her life a living hell before.

"Don't worry, it's bulletproof," Legend promised her.

And he seemed to be correct. The mortars that exploded against its vibrant paint seemed to have no effect at all on the automobile. But then several skidded under the car before they exploded in a rainbow of sparks that bounced the car up off the pavement.

The rest of the crowd streamed through the doors and into the lobby where they watched the disaster unfolding from the safety of the headquarters.

A bald man with a thick Latin accent wearing a shirt that read *Hot Rods Restoration Garage* trotted over to James and patted him on the back. "Don't worry. We can fix it. Just a scratch, I'm sure."

A bunch of other men seemed to concur, until the sparks died down and James asked, "Why is there so much smoke? Does it seem like there's more and more of it instead of less?"

"Uh oh." Tavish hid his laughter behind his hand, which was disturbingly pretty like the rest of him.

Legend groaned and asked one of the guys with the Hot Rods shirts, "When you added that snorkel, didn't you say the car was waterproof?"

They got quiet, their reassurances drying up.

James took his phone out of his pocket and dialed 911. "Yes, we have an automobile fire at Shields Security Services. It's going to require special assistance. Right. It's a waterproof car. Uh huh. Great, thanks."

Before he'd even hung up, sirens wailed. Fortunately, Middletown's firehouse wasn't far away, like most things in the small city. By the time the fire truck flew into the lot practically on two wheels, the car was engulfed in an impressive ball of flames.

"Wow." Karolena whispered, setting off another round of giggles from Tavish.

A group of six firefighters piled out of the truck and started doing their thing as the captain jogged into the building and tipped his hat to one tall man with short-cropped hair. "Hey, Jordan. What's going on? And what the hell is that thing out there?"

"Thanks for coming so fast, Karis."

"It's a perfectly reasonable vehicle." James put his hands on his hips, making everyone launch into another fit of laughter.

In the background, the firefighters' axes bounced off the car windows as they tried to enter and douse the flames. It was no use.

"Sorry about this." Jordan dealt with the fire chief, whom he seemed to be friends—or at least friendly—with, explaining the extensive modifications that had been made to James's car.

"I think it's best if we let it burn itself out then." Karis looked to James and winced. "Sorry 'bout that. But we'll make sure the flames don't spread and hopefully you can get back to your party in an hour or two."

"At least the food is safe!" Legend made an exaggerated swipe across his forehead.

"We've got you, James," a tall guy with tawny hair promised. "Hot Rods don't quit that easy."

"This time you might have met your match, Eli." James's shoulders slumped.

"Nah. It'll be better than ever when we're done with it. Just wait and see."

"What the hell have I gotten myself into?" Karolena muttered beneath her breath, but apparently not low enough to keep Tavish from hearing.

He turned to her with a gorgeous grin. "I wish I could say it's not always this chaotic around here, but I'd be lying."

His partner cracked an equally dazzling smile and something inside her fizzled. *No. Oh no.* She could not afford to be attracted to her new co-workers, who also happened to be her neighbors. Or anyone, for that matter.

She'd already learned the hard way that no amount of hot man and hard cock was worth the trouble. And she had a feeling these two were that and more.

Karolena reminded herself to focus on her goals. She needed a place to lay low. Somewhere safe to sleep while she squirreled away cash so she could come up with a better plan. She hadn't intended to embed herself in a band of hired guns. But maybe it would work out for the best.

"Want me to go out and smuggle some drinks from the food truck?" Tavish asked with bright eyes and a bob of his topknot that in no way came off as innocently friendly. Legend rolled his eyes, which might have been funny for a dark-haired mountain of a man if she'd had any illusions about how dangerous he could be under the right circumstances. "Might as well settle in and enjoy the show."

There were pitfalls here, sure. But anything had to be better than what Karolena had, hopefully, so recently gotten herself out of...assuming Vladimir was really going to let her go. An ominous lurch in Karolena's stomach told her that was even less likely than finding the perfect stronghold to hide from him in. But she had to try to reclaim her life.

Shields was the best chance she had.

For Karolena, Tavish, and Legend's story, read CLAIMED

Jayne is the queen of
ménall partner romance!
CLAIMED
Powertools: The Shields
NEW YORK TIMES & USA TODAY BESTSELLING AUTHOR
JAYNE RYLON

If you'd like to start at the very beginning with the Powertools Crew, you can download a discounted boxset of the first six books HERE.

Yes, I know it says complete series but I wrote a seventh book more recently and haven't gotten around to updating the boxset yet, sorry!

You can find the seventh Powertools book, More the Merrier, HERE.

They are also featured in four books in the Powertools: The Original Crew Returns series starting with Screwed HERE

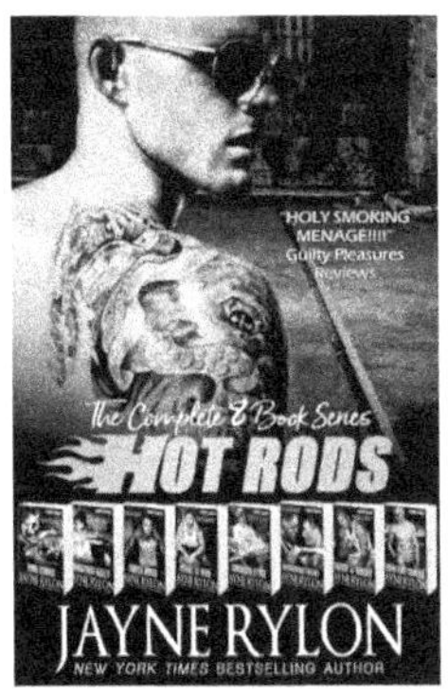

If you missed out on the Powertools: Hot Rods series, you can buy all eight books in a discounted single-volume boxset by clicking HERE.

To read more about the Hot Rides gang, start with Quinn, Trevon, and Devra's story, Wild Ride, click HERE.

CLAIM A $5 GIFT CERTIFICATE

Jayne is so sure you will love her books, she'd like you to try any one of your choosing for free. Claim your $5 gift certificate by signing up for her newsletter. You'll also learn about freebies, new releases, extras, appearances, and more!

www.jaynerylon.com/newsletter

WHAT WAS YOUR FAVORITE PART?

Did you enjoy this book? If so, please leave a review and tell your friends about it. Word of mouth and online reviews are immensely helpful and greatly appreciated.

JAYNE'S SHOP

Check out Jayne's online shop for autographed print
books, direct download ebooks, reading-themed apparel
up to size 5XL, mugs, tote bags, notebooks, Mr. Rylon's
wood (you'll have to see it for yourself!) and more.
www.jaynerylon.com/shop

LISTEN UP!

The majority of Jayne's books are also available in audio format on Audible, Amazon and iTunes.

ABOUT THE AUTHOR

Jayne Rylon is a *New York Times* and *USA Today* bestselling author who has sold more than one million books. She has received numerous industry awards including the Romantic Times Reviewers' Choice Award for Best Indie Erotic Romance and the Swirl Award, which recognizes excellence in diverse romance. She is an Honor Roll member of the Romance Writers of America. Her stories used to begin as daydreams in seemingly endless business meetings, but now she is a full time author, who employs the skills she learned from her straight-laced corporate existence in the business of writing. She lives in Ohio with her husband, the infamous Mr. Rylon, and their cat, Frodo. When she can escape her purple office, she loves to travel the world, avoid speeding tickets in her beloved Sky, SCUBA dive, hunt Pokemon, and–of course–read.

Jayne Loves To Hear From Readers
www.jaynerylon.com
contact@jaynerylon.com
PO Box 10, Pickerington, OH 43147

facebook.com/jaynerylon

twitter.com/JayneRylon

instagram.com/jaynerylon

youtube.com/jaynerylonbooks

bookbub.com/profile/jayne-rylon

amazon.com/author/jaynerylon

ALSO BY JAYNE RYLON

4-EVER

A New Adult Reverse Harem Series

4-Ever Theirs

4-Ever Mine

EVER AFTER DUET

Reverse Harem Featuring Characters From The 4-Ever Series

Fourplay

Fourkeeps

EVER & ALWAYS DUET

Reverse Harem Featuring Characters from the 4-Ever and Ever After Duets

Four Money

Four Love

POWERTOOLS: THE ORIGINAL CREW

Five Guys Who Get It On With Each Other & One Girl. Enough Said?

Kate's Crew

Morgan's Surprise

Kayla's Gift

Devon's Pair

Nailed to the Wall

Hammer it Home

More the Merrier

POWERTOOLS: HOT RODS

Powertools Spin Off. Keep up with the Crew plus...

Seven Guys & One Girl. Enough Said?

King Cobra

Mustang Sally

Super Nova

Rebel on the Run

Swinger Style

Barracuda's Heart

Touch of Amber

Long Time Coming

POWERTOOLS: HOT RIDES

Powertools and Hot Rods Spin Off.

Menage and Motorcycles

Wild Ride

Slow Ride

Hard Ride

Joy Ride

Rough Ride

POWERTOOLS: RETURN OF THE ORIGINAL CREW

The original crew is back with more steamy menage stories!

Screwed

Drilled

Grind

Pound

POWERTOOLS: THE SHIELDS

A group of undercover operatives save the world in these steamy menage stories featuring your other favorite Powertools characters

Found

Lost

Brazen

Broken

Claimed

Shared

MEN IN BLUE

Hot Cops Save Women In Danger

Night is Darkest

Razor's Edge

Mistress's Master

Spread Your Wings

Wounded Hearts

Bound For You

DIVEMASTERS

Sexy SCUBA Instructors By Day, Doms On A Mega-Yacht By Night

Going Down

Going Deep

Going Hard

STANDALONE

Menage

Middleman

Nice & Naughty

Contemporary

Where There's Smoke

Report For Booty

COMPASS BROTHERS

Modern Western Family Drama Plus Lots Of Steamy Sex

Northern Exposure

Southern Comfort

Eastern Ambitions

Western Ties

COMPASS GIRLS

*Daughters Of The Compass Brothers Drive Their Dads Crazy And
Fall In Love*

Winter's Thaw

Hope Springs

Summer Fling

Falling Softly

COMPASS BOYS

Sons Of The Compass Brothers Fall In Love

Heaven on Earth

Into the Fire

Still Waters

Light as Air

PLAY DOCTOR

Naughty Sexual Psychology Experiments Anyone?

Dream Machine

Healing Touch

RED LIGHT

A Hooker Who Loves Her Job

Complete Red Light Series Boxset

FREE - Through My Window - FREE

Star

Can't Buy Love

Free For All

PICK YOUR PLEASURES

Choose Your Own Adventure Romances!

Pick Your Pleasure

Pick Your Pleasure 2

RACING FOR LOVE

MMF Menages With Race-Car Driver Heroes

Complete Series Boxset

Driven

Shifting Gears

PARANORMALS

Vampires, Witches, And A Man Trapped In A Painting

Paranormal Double Pack Boxset

Picture Perfect

Reborn

PENTHOUSE PLEASURES

Naughty Manhattanite Neighbors Find Kinky Love

Taboo

Kinky

Sinner

Mentor

ROAMING WITH THE RYLONS

Non-fiction Travelogues about Jayne & Mr. Rylon's Adventures

Australia and New Zealand